"I need to know if you enjoy working for me,"

Eric Sutter asked. Then he lowered his face toward Courtney's so that they were practically eye–to–eye. "I certainly enjoy working with you."

Courtney backed up. "Of course I do. I like my job."

"Then why did you leave so abruptly last night?" he whispered teasingly. "You hurt my feelings."

"Your . . ." Courtney broke off, her eyes growing wider. She felt the edge of his desk bump up behind her, so that she was now pinned in place.

At that moment, Eric reached out with his hand and caressed her neck. "Don't play games. We don't have time. You knew what was involved when you took this job."

"I have no idea what you're talking about. I took this job because I wanted the experience. The last thing on my mind was getting involved with you. What kind of person do you think I am?"

"I love it." Eric moved toward her again. "You're so full of spirit. You're so beautiful. I know this is just part of your game."

"Stop it!" Courtney suddenly yelled. "Get away from me!"

Don't miss these books
in the exciting FRESHMAN DORM series

Freshman Dorm
Freshman Lies
Freshman Guys
Freshman Nights
Freshman Dreams
Freshman Games
Freshman Loves
Freshman Secrets
Freshman Schemes
Freshman Changes
Freshman Fling
Freshman Rivals
Freshman Heartbreak
Freshman Flames
Freshman Choices
Freshman Feud
Freshman Follies
Freshman Wedding
Freshman Promises
Freshman Summer
Freshman Affair
Freshman Truths

And, coming soon . . .

Freshman Christmas

FRESHMAN SCANDAL

LINDA A. COONEY

HarperPaperbacks
A Division of HarperCollinsPublishers

This is a work of fiction. The characters, incidents, and dialogues are products of the author's imagination and are not to be construed as real. Any resemblance to actual events or persons living or dead, is entirely coincidental.

HarperPaperbacks *A Division of* HarperCollins*Publishers*
10 East 53rd Street, New York, N.Y. 10022

Cover illustration by Tony Greco

First printing: November 1992

Printed in the United States of America

HarperPaperbacks and colophon are trademarks of HarperCollins*Publishers*

❖ 10 9 8 7 6 5 4 3 2

One

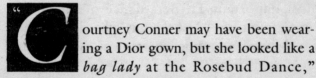

"**C**ourtney Conner may have been wearing a Dior gown, but she looked like a *bag lady* at the Rosebud Dance," Marcia Tabbert hissed. "Her hair and face were a fright."

KC Angeletti bristled. "Don't make jokes about homeless women, Marcia. And don't underestimate Courtney. She's having some kind of problem, but she'll be back on top. You wait."

"I'm not so sure. I pledged Tri Beta last fall because everyone said it was the classiest sorority on campus," another pledge complained softly.

"Courtney was supposed to be this sterling example—"

"Yeah, right," Marcia interjected. "Sterling in need of a lot of polishing."

Courtney drew in her breath sharply and slumped against the wall of the Tri Betas' upstairs hallway. Their Monday morning breakfast meeting had ended a short while ago, but she'd forgotten to remind the freshman pledges about Friday's reception for prominent alumni. Now she didn't want to. The voices coming from the sleeping porch stopped her.

"She actually let herself get stood up for the most important Tri Beta dance of the year," Marcia went on. "And the guy who dumped her was that scruffy-looking reporter with the bandanna she'd been seeing."

Courtney felt her stomach drop like a bowling ball. She wanted to leave. But she didn't. Something made her want to hear the bald truth about how people saw her these days. Maybe it would help her rebuild her life—and her self-respect.

"He was cute," another voice giggled softly. "At least he was better than that hippie she went skinny-dipping with last fall."

"But Courtney embarrassed us all this time,"

someone else reminded them. "She looked tired and unkempt. As the symbolic head of this house, no one else is in a position to set the tone like she is."

"I wish you could hear yourselves talk," Courtney heard KC again. "This is supposed to be a sisterhood, not a church-lady convention."

Courtney sighed. KC was kind, but she wasn't the president of the sorority. Courtney was. She knew her reputation had to be squeaky-clean. She knew she had to put her obsessive relationship with Dash Ramirez behind her forever. She couldn't lose control and throw herself at him anymore. It was time to accept the fact that Dash wasn't interested in her—time to pull the threads of her life back together.

Straightening up and smoothing the velvet band that held back her shiny blond hair, Courtney finally headed down the carpeted hall and descended the oak staircase.

Everyone knows how crazy I've been, and they're all watching and waiting for me to collapse, she thought. *But I'm not going to. I'm going to hold my head high. For the next few months, I will eat, sleep and breathe work. And I'm not going to even glance at another guy until summer vacation.*

Courtney stopped briefly in the Tri Betas' stately

entryway, and fiddled nervously with the tabs on her leather organizer. Then she felt a hand on her shoulder and turned around. Dressed in a crisp, white blouse and a tailored skirt, KC had a look of patient optimism that immediately lifted Courtney's spirits.

"Hi," KC began, her gray eyes fixed on Courtney curiously. As always, KC's erect posture and slim body made her clothes look like they were bought at a ritzy boutique, even though they were carefully selected from secondhand stores and discount department chains. "I've got a nine o'clock. Are you headed toward campus too?"

"Sure." Courtney gave her a grateful smile. "I've got an appointment in the Forsythe Building. Let's walk over together."

"How is everything?" KC asked casually as they headed outside onto Greek Row, a pleasant, leafy avenue lined with stately mansions and manicured lawns.

Courtney stiffened a little. The subject of Dash had never really come up between them and she still wasn't ready to open up.

"Fine," Courtney said, giving KC a friendly pat on the back. She tilted her head teasingly in KC's direction. "Well, let's see. Except for the freshman pledges breathing down my neck over weekend curfews, the hoard of incredibly successful Tri Beta alumni about to descend on us, an international economics exam tomorrow, and a big report due in ten minutes, I'm okay."

KC smiled, then frowned as a convertible stuffed with fraternity guys sailed by and whistled loudly. "Why do they have to do that?" KC complained.

Courtney shrugged. "Ignore them. It's harmless."

"It's demeaning."

"Hey," Courtney changed the subject. "I know I've been a little out of it lately. Thanks for being patient."

KC shrugged, grinning happily, swinging her huge leather briefcase. "You've been there for me."

"What are friends for?" Courtney nudged KC with her elbow. "You look happy, by the way. I think meeting your natural mother for the first time was good for you. Or maybe it's that gorgeous, tall Cody Wainwright you've been seeing."

KC smiled and raked her long dark hair back with a hand. "Maybe it's a little of both. But we're still talking about you. What's it like to intern for one of the country's top financial wizards? Is he really smart enough to pull the U of S out of financial doldrums?"

"Doldrums?" Courtney grinned. Just thinking

about her internship with the brilliant economist Eric Sutter made her feel like she was walking on firmer ground. He'd recently arrived on campus to help the University of Springfield board of regents deal with an emergency budget shortfall. And Courtney had immediately landed a prestigious internship with him.

"Is he as impressive as he sounds on paper?"

Courtney nodded, her heels clicking briskly up the path to campus. "He's an incredible person. Organized. To the point. Articulate."

KC nodded seriously. "Yeah. I read that he's advised the White House and several state legislatures. Yale graduate. Stanford MBA. Only twenty-nine years old and his views are published in *Time* and *The Economist*. He's going to be a great connection for you someday."

Courtney stopped where the path branched off toward the Forsythe Building. "Thanks, KC. I'm starting to feel good about things."

KC waved cheerfully at a group of fellow business-class students scurrying toward Parker Hall. "So— what's this report about? Is it for Sutter?"

A thrill of pride went up Courtney's spine. "Well —yes, actually. It's on the possible implications of cuts and tuition increases."

KC's face dropped. "Tuition increases? I can

barely afford college now. A tuition hike will turn me into a dropout."

"Don't worry yet," Courtney said, patting KC's shoulder. "I'm sure Eric will do everything he can to avoid that."

"I'll try. But let me know whatever you hear."

Courtney watched her friend head down the path, then turned purposefully in the direction of the ancient Forsythe Building. The smell of freshly cut grass hung in the air, and a few students were lazily throwing a Frisbee back and forth across the dorm green.

Clutching her report tightly to her chest, Courtney entered the building and took the elevator to the third floor, where Eric Sutter had set up temporary offices. Someone had gone to a lot of trouble over the weekend to tastefully decorate the cramped quarters. Several lush potted plants stood in the corners of the outer office, and an elegant oriental rug had been thrown down over the gray commercial carpeting. Courtney closed the frosted-glass door and waved quietly to a couple of guys in pinstriped shirts, pressed pants, and tasseled loafers, who looked up briefly from a computer screen filled with numbers and charts.

"Give me a break, Stevenson," one of the interns

hissed. "You can't run these numbers unless you have linkage with a System-7 application."

Courtney frowned and looked down at the folder containing her detailed report on rescuing the university from its financial squeeze. She knew it was going to take more than fancy computers and complicated number charts to solve the university's problems.

"You've been working too hard." Eric Sutter interrupted her thoughts. He was leaning casually against the door to the inner office, his hands in his pockets, staring at her silently. The blue of his oxford button-down shirt brought out the deep blue of his eyes and contrasted handsomely with his blond hair. "I've got a sister going for her Wharton MBA. So I know that look."

Courtney smiled. "Things have been pretty busy lately. But I finished the report you asked for."

Eric nodded vigorously. "Good. I've got a few minutes. Come in"

Courtney followed him, dumbfounded. She couldn't believe he was going to look at the report now.

"Hefty," he muttered, taking the report from her. "Coffee?"

Courtney slipped into a seat and tucked her legs beneath the chair. "No, thank you," she murmured, watching with satisfaction as he flipped the report open and began reading it.

"Uh huh. Mmm."

She glanced about the office, which was also decorated with plants, cleverly framed cartoons, and small oriental rugs. In the corner of Eric's desk stood a photo of him posing with the President of the United States in front of an American flag.

The phone rang and Courtney could see one of its buttons blinking.

"Hey, Trevor," Eric cupped his hands and called into the outer office. "Pick that one up for me, and please close my door." He gave Courtney a knowing look as the door thumped shut. "Got to give these guys something to do, or they'll play computer games all day." He shrugged and flashed her a smile. "Okay, it's my own fault. Trevor's dad gave me a call and *voila*, he's an instant intern. But then, Trevor's dad is the Secretary of Commerce."

Courtney laughed and gave him a sheepish smile.

He held one of her charts up at an angle, nodded, closed the report, and slipped it onto his desk thoughtfully. Then he leaned back in his chair and sighed. "I like your numbers on the 1975 tuition

hikes and aid cutbacks. Makes sense. Three percent enrollment drop. Up five percent the next
year. Short-term recovery. Sports revenues intact."

Courtney nodded.

"Your research on the implications of an inten-
sive private endowment fund drive is excellent, and
I like your point about a higher-profile effort to
set up the industry-funded chairs in more of the
hard-science departments. It's been a neglected
long-term cost-saving angle. Not to mention the
impact it could have on attracting East Coast hot-
shots and upping enrollment."

Courtney's head was whirring. Eric had spent
barely three minutes glancing at her report, but
he'd completely absorbed the data and was already
discussing it with her.

Eric leaned forward and tiredly propped his chin
up on his fists. "Trouble is, the university wouldn't
be in the mire it's in today if the regents had taken
your advice ten, or even five, years ago."

"Yes, but . . ."

"Your ideas will be in my recommendation, but
we're going to have to propose some short-term
solutions as well." Eric straightened up in his
chair. He crossed his legs casually and looked at
her as he took a sip of coffee from a mug that read
Yale in black-and-white lettering.

Courtney could hardly believe it. Here she was, a junior in college, barely recovered from an hysterical, obsessive relationship, and already one of the nation's top economists was going to use one of her recommendations.

"Short-term means either program cuts or tuition hikes," Eric said, shaking his head. Then he gave her an intense look. "What do you think should be done?"

Courtney coughed. "Well, actually, my research has turned up some fairly well-padded programs —particularly in the athletic departments . . ."

"Whoa," Eric protested, smiling and holding up his hands. His tanned face had a sort of healthy gleam to it that reminded Courtney of the guys who used to hang out at her parents' tennis club back home. "What made me so sure you would say that?"

"Well, it's true," Courtney began, nervously fingering the edge of her notebook. "Look at the two hundred thousand dollars spent on thermal seats for the stadium. And the—"

"Come on, Courtney," Eric complained good-naturedly. "Alumni get arthritis—and worse." He chuckled. "You know as well as I do that university athletic departments are gold mines. Both in ticket sales and alumni goodwill. I say we go with a modest tuition hike and leave the athletic money machines alone."

He slid his elbow out to the side so it rested lazily on his desk. "Look at it this way," he joked. "Most of these students wouldn't know the difference if their tuition went up a few percentage points. They know Mom and Pop will fork it over."

Courtney frowned. She thought of KC, who had to struggle for every penny that went toward her tuition and books. A tuition hike might mean that she'd have to leave school. And what about the hundreds, maybe thousand of others who couldn't rely on wealthy parents?

"I think you're wrong," Courtney said calmly. She looked across at Eric, reminding herself that she hadn't made the honor roll and gotten this prestigious internship by acting like a frightened mouse. "A large percentage of students rely on federal aid, work-study grants and even high-percentage bank loans to finance their college education," Courtney continued, taking the report off his desk and checking the statistics on the back page. "You'll turn them into dropouts if you raise tuition."

"But—"

"Sure," Courtney interrupted, noticing that

Eric was beginning to look at her seriously. "Sure, athletic-department cutbacks are going to anger a certain constituency. But I say you go with across-the-board cuts and no tuition increases. No favors for athletes. Let everyone tighten their belt equally."

There was a long silence. Courtney looked steadily back at Eric, whose jaw had begun to twitch slightly. And though his face was slightly red, he still hadn't taken his eyes off her.

"You're right," he finally said, looking down. His eyes lifted up again and he smiled. "I hate it when other people are so right."

Courtney felt herself blushing a little.

"If we cut everyone equally there would be fewer complaints," Eric continued. He leaned back in his chair with his hands behind his neck. "But what would happen, of course, is that everyone would complain. Still, I'm going to think about what you've said." Eric thoughtfully twisted the band on his gold watch. "Thanks for having the guts to tell me what you really think. Are you always this disagreeable?"

"Only when I'm talking about money," Courtney tossed back.

Eric smiled. "I want to make you an offer."

"Oh?"

"The board of regents wants me to choose a student who'll act as liaison between them and the student body during these cutback talks," Eric explained. "I'd like to offer the job to you, Courtney."

Courtney was so startled, she didn't answer.

"You can take a day or so to think it over," Eric said. "But you've worked harder and thought more carefully than any of the other interns. You'll get a class credit and a grade from me. And your first assignment would be to help me field questions from the audience after my first speech to the student body this week. What do you say?"

"Think it over?" Courtney breathed happily. "Of course I'll take the job. Thank you very much."

She reached out and shook Eric's outstretched hand. Then she looked down, blushed, and released it with a laugh.

Eric looked down and laughed too. "That's okay. A little extended handshaking never hurt a tired economist like me."

Courtney backed slowly out the door. "Thanks again. I hope I can help."

"I have no doubts about you, Courtney," he replied, still looking at her approvingly. "No doubts whatsoever."

Courtney closed the door quietly behind her

and realized that she had been holding her breath. Then she let it out with a half laugh, half cry of pure joy.

"Good-bye, Dash. Good-bye crazy, lost self. I'm on my way at last," she whispered to herself as the two male interns exchanged glances. Courtney smiled at them, then headed to the elevator.

For all I know, I could make it to the top, she thought, pushing the down button. *Why not Chairman of the Board? Why not the White House?*

Two

....

"Nickel-and-dime coverage," Dash Ramirez said with disgust, ripping a page of news and feature copy out of the *U of S Weekly Journal*'s national wire-service printer. His scraggly hair was flopped over his forehead, and his ink-stained gray T-shirt drooped over his faded jeans.

KRUS disk jockey Cody Wainwright replied with a short laugh, bending his tall frame over a tiny fax machine at the other end of the room. His dark brown hair was tied loosely back, and his high cheekbones rose above a row of white teeth.

"Yeah, you could write that stuff in your sleep."

It was Monday afternoon in the *Journal*'s fax-photocopy cave, crammed under a staircase just off the newsroom's basement offices. Dash shoved aside a pile of balled-up candy wrappers and flopped down on a folding chair.

"State Patrol Urges Caution on Rain-slick Roads!" Dash read with mock surprise, his ankle nervously bobbing up and down on his knee.

"Whoa!" Cody pretended to stagger backward.

"Cookbook Author Inspired by European Sojourns!"

"No. Tell me it ain't so!" Cody continued to joke in his soft, Tennessee drawl.

"Whew. Real thumb-suckers." Dash shook his head. "There's supposed to be something breaking in D.C. over federal student-loan cuts. We could use it as a tie-in to that upcoming Eric Sutter proposal."

"But noooo," Cody added, rolling his eyes. The fax machine began its familiar screeching noise and he twisted his neck around to see what it was spitting out. "I could use a student-loan story too. Talk about a dead news day. And I've got a three o'clock news spot coming up in less than an hour."

"Drag," Dash agreed, sinking his forehead onto

his fist. In ten minutes, *Journal* editor-in-chief, Greg Sukamaki would be holding a staff meeting in the main office.

For the last couple of weeks, Dash had been busting his brain covering the university's financial woes—currently the *Journal*'s top news story. So far, he'd done a couple of interviews and a background piece on visiting consultant and financial whiz kid Eric Sutter. He'd also dug up some past U of S investment blunders and even a few personality conflicts among the board of regents.

Still, Dash didn't know what Greg thought of his work. He didn't even know if Greg would keep him on the story. Things had been too crazy and distracting for him over the last week. His long-delayed and totally bizarre breakup with Tri Beta president Courtney Conner had sapped him.

Cody sat down on a desk and stretched his long legs out in front of him. "This one's for you, Ramirez," he said, reading the faxed copy. "News flash from the dorm-residents' association: Coleridge Hall residents will begin a co-ed roommate experiment next week. *Co-ed by bed.*"

"Huh?" Dash knitted his eyebrows.

"Says here everyone's going to be assigned a roommate of the opposite sex for a week."

"That'll be a trip," Dash said. "Count me out. Just give me my solitary dive."

"Whew, you're not joshin'," Cody agreed. "Oh, and here's another item. The dorm association reports that the thefts of cash have apparently stopped. But the thief was never found."

Dash clenched his jaw. "There are enough minor-league stories on this campus to stretch to the moon and back," he snapped, stabbing the air with his finger. "And if Sukamaki decides I'm his man for a bunch of puff pieces about trading beds and snatched purses, I'm outta here."

"What's the problem?" Cody asked, looking down at him quizzically. "Your editor wants you free for the budget-crunch story, doesn't he?"

Dash shrugged and had a sudden, desperate need for a cigarette. He reached instinctively for his back pocket, then remembered he'd quit a while ago. Instead, he raked his fingers anxiously through his hair. "I'm not so sure. Ever since sorority princess Courtney Conner started hanging around the *Journal* office, everyone looks at me differently."

"Guess it just ripped your hell-raiser reputation into tiny little pieces," Cody said laughing. "Your newsroom buddies must think you're turning soft.

Or going crazy. Hey, you were messin' with your stereotype, Ramirez. No fair."

Dash shook his head. "Don't I know it."

Cody continued to look at him quietly from his position on the desk. He shifted uncomfortably. "So," he said cautiously. "What *are* you doing with Courtney?"

"Well . . ." Dash began in confusion. "I don't know. She came on to me. I took the bait. I mean —God—she was unbelievably gorgeous. We saw each other a few times, and then she went crazy on me. Wouldn't take no for an answer. At the end, I had to practically scream in her ear: *Don't come near me!*"

"Nasty. The reason I ask," Cody ventured, rising up from the desk and folding his arms across his chest, "is because KC Angeletti is a good friend of hers."

"Yeah," Dash replied. "Smart. No princess-type. Gutsy, I'd say. You seeing her?"

"Yes," Cody replied, looking steadily ahead. He fingered the carved silver bracelet that was clasped around his forearm. "But it's a little vague right now. I like her a lot. There's just a loose end in the way."

"Another guy?"

"Peter Dvorsky. Know him?"

"Yeah. Good guy. Straightforward. Got a free ticket to shoot pictures in Italy—the bum," Dash said enviously. "Have you asked KC about him?"

Cody smiled, a distant look in his eye. "It's not that easy. Let's just say KC doesn't let go of her secrets. But I need to know how she feels."

"I think I know what you mean," Dash said quietly, ducking his head into the newsroom. Cody had hit a nerve. Dash, too, was struggling with the mysterious mind of his ex-girlfriend, Lauren Turnbell-Smythe. But there wasn't enough time to start talking about that now. "Gotta go. Talk to you later about this. The meeting's already started."

"Yeah." Cody followed him. "I've got a communications class in five minutes."

Dash walked into the cluttered newsroom and took his place on an overturned garbage can by the water cooler. By this time, the place was filled with an assortment of reporter-types, ranging from burly Joe Eddy, who edited the sports pages, to wiry-haired Alison Albright, one of the *Journal*'s top investigative reporters.

"Where's Princess-C., Dash?" A guy in the back laughed.

"Here she comes, Miss Ameri-ca," Alison hummed loudly.

"Where are your golf clubs, big guy?" Joe called out. "Miss Manners is gonna want you to play with her daddy."

Dash glared briefly at the group, then looked away, only to meet Lauren's violet eyes in midair. He looked at her nervously as she leaned against a pillar on the other side of the room. He and Lauren had broken up a few months ago, after she claimed he'd tried to take full credit for an investigative journalism piece they'd written together. It had all been a misunderstanding, but Lauren refused to come around.

Dash clenched his jaw. For a moment, he thought he saw a flicker of longing and pain in her gaze. Is that what it was? There was no way he could be sure.

"Okay, everybody," Greg was saying distractedly. "May I have your attention?"

Dash tried to look at Greg, but his eyes kept darting across the room to where Lauren was standing.

Wearing a white shirt tucked into a pair of jeans, she looked great. Even better than she had looked when they were together. Her hair was different —combed into soft waves. And, what was it? Wasn't she a lot thinner, too? He could see the beautiful bones in her face.

All he wanted to do was walk over to her and bury his face in her neck. He wanted nothing more than to be with her again.

"Ramirez?" Greg was saying. Dash looked to the front of the room. The entire group was staring at him, smirking.

"Uh, yeah?"

Greg put his hand on his hip and sighed. "Dash, you're a space cadet, but you're doing a helluva job on this budget story. I'm even going to give you some help. I think I want another body on this."

Dash watched Greg's eyes roam the room and fix on Lauren. "Lauren, I want you on the numbers," he said nonchalantly. "Dash, you stick with the political stuff."

A warm thread of hope began winding its way through Dash. But when he glanced back at Lauren, she was giving him a so-what look.

"Okay, folks," Greg barked. "I want as much copy as possible by tonight. If you're filing a story Tuesday morning, it better be breaking news. And it better be good."

Slowly, Dash edged his way across the room to where Lauren was now sitting behind a desk, jotting something down in a notebook. He looked at the way her hair fell over her face. Somehow it reminded him of the winter before, when she'd curl up in his ancient, overstuffed chair, her head bent over a novel or a volume of short stories. Dash sighed. Back then, he had no idea how lucky he was.

Lauren looked up casually from her writing.

"Say," Dash began awkwardly, touching the edge of her desk with his fingertip. "Since we'll be working together on the Eric Sutter stuff, I thought we could use the material for a 'His/Her' column," he stammered. He and Lauren had started the column when they were a couple. Now it was one of the hottest reads in the paper, even though they barely spoke to each other about it.

"Maybe," Lauren answered, her pencil poised in midair.

Dash glanced back over his shoulder to make sure no one was listening. The room had emptied out and they were practically alone. Desperately, he tried to think of something to say, just so he could be near her. He slid his hip onto the edge of her desk. "So—uh—how's Melissa? You still spending a lot of time with her?"

Lauren leaned back in her chair and began fiddling with her pencil. Melissa McDormand was Lauren's roommate, still brokenhearted over her aborted wedding to Brooks Baldwin.

"Not really," Lauren said coolly. "I thought I could help her. But now I think she's the only one who can pull herself out of her depression. And so far, I'm not sure she wants to."

Dash shook his head. "It must be lousy."

"Yeah." Lauren gave him a challenging stare. "Men are capable of pulling some pretty nasty tricks."

Dash shifted nervously.

"I don't know," Lauren continued, crossing her arms across her chest. "Melissa can't sit in our room moping and eating junk food for the rest of her life. She's a brilliant premed student on a track scholarship. How can she face herself? I think she should talk to Winnie."

"That's a good idea," Dash said faintly. Winnie Gottlieb was a psych major who worked at the Crisis Hotline. Dash didn't really want to talk about Melissa and Winnie, but at least Lauren was talking to him.

"I mean," Lauren continued thoughtfully, "I can't spend all my time trying to cheer up people who don't want to help themselves. I have my *own* life to live. Classes. My writing. My work at the *Journal*. I'm even signed up for a self-defense class in two weeks."

Dash's eyes opened wide. He'd never seen

quiet, refined Lauren so confident. Even brash. She's always been calm, forgiving, and unselfish— to the extreme. It was as if she'd gone through a personality change. "Sounds good, Lauren," Dash whispered.

"Yeah," Lauren replied with a sudden smile. "I'm doing twenty-five laps a night at the U pool and writing for at least two solid hours a day. It's amazing what you can accomplish if you forget everything else and focus on yourself."

She stood up and checked her watch.

"You leaving?" Dash asked.

"Yep. I have a creative-writing class in ten minutes."

Dash began to follow her toward the door, his hands in his pockets. It was almost as if their old roles had been reversed. Suddenly, he was the insecure puppy dog and she was the confident, self-absorbed writer with a mission. "So—uh—do you want to do the 'His/Her' column with me on the budget?"

She paused, looked at him, and shrugged. "I guess so. Why don't you meet me at Sutter's speech conference on Wednesday in the student union? We'll dream up an angle and go from there."

"Okay."

"Bye," Lauren said shortly, turning and stepping briskly out the door.

Dash slumped down in the nearest chair. Maybe he was totally crazy to want her still. She obviously didn't want *him*. But his emotionless fling with Courtney had made him realize that Lauren was the one for him. He wanted to get back together. No matter what the cost. No matter what he had to do.

Three
································

innie Gottlieb held a book in her hand as she dumped a bowl of scrambled eggs in the hot frying pan the next morning.

While the yellow mixture bubbled and curled at the edges, Winnie continued to read and bob up and down at the same time. Her short dark hair was spiked out in all directions, and her green satin bathrobe was covered with pictures of 1950's-era women dancing with fruit bowls on their heads.

"My life," she read in a mock-serious voice, "is a story of the self-realization of the unconscious."

"Huh?" Her new husband, Josh Gaffey, looked up as he chopped a bell pepper next to a large mound of sliced tomatoes. "What did you say?"

Winnie closed the book and slapped it down on the kitchen counter. She gave Josh a warm smile and began happily stirring the eggs in the pan. "Oh, nothing. Just the words of Carl Jung, famous Swiss psychoanalyst. We're studying him for the next two weeks in my psych class. I love him already."

"And I love you," Josh murmured, twisting the pepper around and chopping it in the other direction. Wearing a pair of sweats and a white T-shirt with the sleeves ripped off, he looked more like a gentle member of a motorcycle gang than one of the university's top computer brains. His dark hair was cut close in back, but flopped over his eyes in the front. There was a tiny blue stone in one ear.

"I love you, too."

"And roo-tee-too-too."

"And loopy loo-loo."

A guy with dark curly hair, wearing jeans and a plaid pajama top, strolled in, smiling shyly. "B–break it up," he said with his gentle stutter. "I know you've only been married a few weeks. B-but you could possibly get on my nerves one day."

"You and Clifford agreed to the off-campus

house share, Rich," Winnie teased him good-naturedly. "No backing out now."

Rich Greenberg slid awkwardly into a seat near the kitchen table and smiled. "I'm not backing out. I'm just about to sample the famous breakfast b–burritos you two have been bragging about."

"No problemo," Winnie joked, chopping the eggs up and checking the tortillas in the oven. She straightened up and looked around with satisfaction at their funky, 1930's kitchen, complete with salmon-pink tile trimmed in cherry red. She liked the old-fashioned glass cabinets and the hardwood floors that ran throughout the four-bedroom shingle house.

She and Josh couldn't have afforded the place on their own. They only lived here because their friend, Clifford Bronton, had discovered it and made them an offer they couldn't refuse. Now she and Josh and Rich and Clifford were getting along better than she'd dreamed. For the last few weeks, they'd been painting the upstair rooms every night and furnishing them with cast-off junk they found in secondhand stores and abandoned next to university dumpsters.

"You are the sunshine of my liiiiiife," Winnie sang off-key, slipping the eggs into a bowl and setting them next to Josh's vegetables.

"Oh, stop." Rich put his hands over his ears while Josh chuckled.

Winnie sighed with happiness. It was one of her jokes. She'd pick a corny song and sing it slightly out of tune. It drove most people crazy, but not Josh. He always laughed. Everything was perfect and wonderful. Her psych classes. Her new life with Josh. Her housemates. Her Crisis Hotline work.

Rich stood up and leaned his lanky frame over the counter. "Hey, Josh. Do you have desktop publishing capability?"

"Here we go again," Winnie said good-naturedly, slapping placemats and napkins down on the table. Her chunky neon bracelets clattered on her slim arms. "Computer talk. Go ahead. Nerd out. Don't mind me. Just pretend I'm a potted philodendron. Or a spoon. Or a bottle of dishwashing liquid. Or a paper clip. Or a . . ."

"Win," Josh said.

"Okay."

"Yeah, I do," Josh turned back to Rich. "I've got design software, four ram, eighty megahertz, a laser printer, and a bunch of computer clip-art."

Rich shifted his elbows on the counter. Winnie saw that his eyes had an eager glitter in them.

"Uh —well—could you give me a hand with it? I want to make up some—uh—good-luck stationery for Liza."

Winnie hoisted herself up on the counter next to the stove and slipped her hands under her knees. Liza Ruff was the wacky, comedienne roommate of her best friend, Faith Crowley. Liza had recently won a U of S comedy contest and on Friday would appear on a live national cable-television show, *Laugh . . . Or Else.*

"Sure thing, Rich," Josh replied. "I've got some time tonight."

"How nice," Winnie agreed. "Liza is lucky to have you."

Rich smiled. "She's also lucky because she's not going to have to travel. The cable company decided to make it a live broadcast from the U of S theater-arts building."

"Cool. We'll be there," Winnie said. "I just wish that you could have been in the contest too, Rich. That was such a rotten deal when some jerk stole the dummy you needed for your ventriloquist act."

Winnie thought she saw something hard and bitter cross Rich's face, but it disappeared in an instant. "Yeah," he came back. "Tough break. But at least I found Liza."

"You two sure make a good couple," Winnie said softly.

"Thanks. After Friday, Liza will know how I really feel about her."

"Rich," Winnie sighed, "I think you're in love."

"I just want to make it a night she'll never forget."

Winnie laughed. "More like Friday will be unforgettable for everyone who sees Liza. Her flame-red hair. Her outrageous clothes. Her amazingly voluptuous figure. That girl's gonna be a star."

"Oh, a big star," Rich said softly.

"Talk about realizing what's in your unconscious," Winnie chattered on. "Carl Jung would have loved her. She's so spontaneous on stage, you know she's tapping into her unconscious. Actors and comedians are totally together that way. They have secret powers."

"Actors are crazy," Josh cracked. "Comedians are worse. No offense, Rich."

"Josh!" Winnie laughed, then stopped. She looked down from her perch on the counter and watched as the floor began to wobble beneath her. For a second, she thought an earthquake had hit Springfield, but then she could barely hold her head up, she was so dizzy. "Josh?" Winnie mumbled, swaying to the right.

"Win!" she heard Josh cry out as she tumbled to the floor, snagging the frying pan with her arm on the way down.

"*Ahhhhh,*" Winnie screamed. The hot pan had burned her arm, and she'd bumped the side of her thigh into the sharp edge of one of the kitchen chairs.

Swiftly, Josh slipped his arms around her and cradled her on the floor, against his chest. "Winnie!" he cried. "Are you okay? Winnie? Did you burn yourself?"

Winnie could feel Rich sliding the chair out of her way. "You really whacked your leg."

"Yeah," Winnie said, lifting herself up halfway to get a better look at her injuries. Tears were smarting in her eyes. She rubbed the numb side of her leg and looked at the triangle-shaped burn on her arm. "Leave it to me to ruin a perfectly fine morning. I don't know what happened."

"What *did* happen, Win?" Josh asked her. He crouched down next to her. Winnie stared at his terrified expression.

"I'm okay, Josh. Really I am. I just got a little dizzy." Then she smiled up at Rich. "Must have been all our talk about love that made me swoon."

The phone suddenly rang and Josh picked it up. "Yeah?" he barked into the receiver. There was a pause and Josh looked exasperated. "Oh, hi. Uh. Just a minute." Josh put his hand over the receiver and narrowed his eyebrows. "It's Melissa. She says she really needs to talk to you."

Winnie rubbed her leg and tried to remember where they'd put the burn ointment. "Tell her I've just taken a little spill," she whispered. "Tell her to meet me at the Crisis Hotline. I'll be there tomorrow afternoon and Thursday, too."

Winnie limped over to a nearby chair and examined her burn while Josh made the explanation and hung up. He put his hand on his hip. "Melissa sounds bad. But I'm more worried about you, Win."

Rich, who had ducked into the freezer for some ice cubes, returned with an ice pack. "Put this on your b-burn for a few minutes."

Winnie looked back and forth between the two guys, who were staring at her as if she were a stranger from the fifth dimension.

She burst out laughing. "Please don't make a big deal about it. It's probably just my unconscious revealing itself."

"Huh?" Josh and Rich said in unison.

Winnie looked at them. "You know. Your unconscious telling you what you're supposed to do."

Josh crossed his arms and looked amused. "So what is it telling you to do?"

"I'm not sure," Winnie replied, resting her chin on her finger. "I'll figure it out if you give me enough time."

Four
....

"**I** need a three-pronged extension cord at least twenty feet long immediately," Courtney said to a student-union staffer.

She quickly checked her clipboard one last time as dozens of students, faculty members, and guys in athletic jackets began pouring through the doors of the student union's vast Cedarwood Room early Wednesday evening.

In fifteen minutes, Eric Sutter would unveil a daring financial plan to the student body. And it hadn't come easily.

Over the last few days, she and Eric had downed cup after cup of coffee together preparing for it.

Courtney had wrangled data out of a Washington bureaucrat on family incomes, and had dug up an important national study on athletic-program revenues. Eric had been so impressed and ecstatic by her hard work that he'd practically kissed her with joy.

"Whew. Extension cord is in place," the student-union staffer said, coming back. "You were right about needing the bigger sound system and taking out the room partitions."

"Mmm-mmm," Courtney said absently, tugging the strap on the tape recorder slung around her shoulder. "Sound system, check. Water, check. Podium mike, check. Eric Sutter introduction notes, check."

Courtney looked up and felt a rush of exhilaration zip through her body. There had been a lot of boring details to take care of, but her last week with Eric had been like a crash course in high finance. Interest rates. Endowment funds. Debt restructuring. She wasn't just Courtney Conner-college-junior-taking-classes-and-setting-up-tea-parties-for-her-sorority. All of a sudden she was involved in something much bigger. Her research could affect the lives of thousands of students. Her new contacts could influence her career for years to come.

Just then, Courtney saw a new wave of people come in. One person in particular caught her eye. "Dash!" she whispered to herself.

Across the room, Dash Ramirez was huddling with a group of reporters who were bent over one of the fact sheets Courtney had prepared for the meeting. She could see Dash's familiar ragged jeans. His black T-shirt beneath his scruffy tweed jacket. His red bandanna tied around his neck. His disheveled black hair. She started again when she saw Lauren standing next to him in a funky Chinese jacket, her soft head of hair bent close to his. Courtney suddenly felt as if someone had thrown scrap metal into her smooth-running mind.

"Get me some more chairs in the back," she called out to the staffer. The room was already nearly full, and the noise was deafening. Several students were holding handmade protest signs, and the entire U of S football team had shown up, complete with uniforms, helmets, and menacing looks.

Courtney knew she had to steel herself. She had to blot Dash out of her mind, get to the podium, and introduce Eric before the crowd got out of hand. Carefully, she pushed her way through the sea of bodies until she reached the microphone, which was positioned on a stage slightly above the milling crowd.

"Ah—hem," Courtney cleared her throat. She adjusted the microphone down and gazed steadily out at the hundreds of concerned faces jamming the room. "Good afternoon. My name is Courtney Conner, and I'm serving as the U of S student body's official liaison to the board during these important budget talks. I've—"

"Who appointed you?" someone called from the back of the room. Courtney's heart sank. It was Dash.

"Uh, excuse me, but . . ." Courtney stammered.

"I'm Dash Ramirez from the *Journal*," Dash said coldly. "You say you represent the student body, but I don't remember any election."

"Yeah!" a student called out. "Who ran against you?"

A loud wave of murmurs and exclamations rushed over her. Courtney braced herself. It was as if her whole future depended upon her performance at this meeting. She wasn't going to let anyone rattle her.

Even Dash.

Especially Dash.

"I was appointed by the board of regents' representative, Eric Sutter," Courtney began smoothly.

"Oh, you mean the regents' high-paid financial and political consultant?" Dash called. "Why is *he* deciding who will represent students?"

Courtney tried in vain to relax her shoulders under her dark blue gabardine suit. She could almost feel her gold earrings shaking against her skin, and thought for a moment she was capable of actually running out of the room. Dash had a point and she knew it. Instead, she fixed a professional smile on her face and mentally cemented it in place.

"Glad you asked," she replied coolly. "That way I can begin the introductions. Ladies and gentlemen, the U of S has been fortunate enough to acquire the services of Mr. Eric Sutter, whose Denver financial-consulting firm has been a leader in—"

"We want to know where all the money went!" a beefy-looking guy wearing a U of S football booster hat yelled.

"Yeah, we want some answers now," Dash called.

"I—I, uh," Courtney began to stammer. The situation was getting completely out of control. Her mouth was getting dry and she suddenly forgot everything she was supposed to say.

Then she felt a warm hand on her shoulder.

She looked around and saw that Eric was standing

next to her. "Relax," he whispered. "Don't let the wolves see you sweat." He removed his perfectly cut suit jacket, draped it on a nearby chair, then rolled up his sleeves.

Courtney stepped back a little and looked into his eyes. She could barely believe how cool Eric was under pressure. She watched as he ducked his his head down to the mike and smiled confidently at the crowd. "To heck with the introduction, folks. It's not vital, anyway. It's time to get to *work*."

"All right!" someone yelled from the crowd.

Courtney took a seat on the stage and gazed victoriously at Dash, who glanced at her briefly. Then, as if to show her new role—worthy of his respect—she turned her eyes toward Eric and didn't look at Dash again.

"Folks, let me start by saying that the university is having financial problems because of two things: state and federal funding has been cut, and it's not earning as much interest on its investments as it has in the past."

Courtney watched the mood of the crowd turn quiet and serious. Several students were nodding their heads in agreement, and a few of the protest signs dropped down.

"There's no conspiracy. There are no real villains

here, except maybe the politicians you did or didn't vote for," Eric continued smoothly. A few bursts of laughter rose from the room.

"What the university needs now is some tight-fisted financial control," Eric urged, leaning forward on the podium. Courtney proudly watched his penetrating stare roam the audience. "And everyone—everyone—is going to have to bite the bullet. At least temporarily."

A girl with frizzy hair and a protest sign stood up angrily. "Everyone except the meatheads who play ball for the alumni, you mean," she shouted.

"Actually," Eric said firmly, glancing down at a sheet of figures he'd brought with him. "That's not what I'm proposing."

There was a murmur in the crowd.

"I say the university must cut back for the next two years. But not selectively. I'm talking across-the-board cuts in all departments. Including the athletic department. Everyone must share the burden. The only other choice is to raise tuition. And that's out of the question."

Courtney beamed with pride. Eric had used the very same plan she'd proposed. He was even using her language.

Eric bent down over the microphone. "Courtney has fact sheets available if you'd like more information about the plan. And we have another meeting Saturday that will deal with the athletic budgets. Any questions?"

"You bet I have some questions!" a guy in a football uniform swaggered toward Courtney as she stepped tentatively down from the platform. "The sports program keeps this university alive. We bring in the dough."

"You can take your fact sheet and smoke it," a guy with an earring in his nose yelled, shaking his fist.

Suddenly, Courtney saw that the swelling crowd, now standing, was actually being forced down the aisle by the angry people in the back. In a split second, the room had become a threatening mass of writhing, shouting bodies, all pressing forward.

Courtney glanced back for a safe exit. She didn't see one, but she felt someone step on her foot. Just as she was about to slump down in pain, a supporting hand lifted her by the arm.

"Steady," Eric said. "Things are out of hand. Follow me."

Courtney nodded, following him out the back door, where a car was waiting in a dark parking lot. Eric pulled out his keys, and Courtney noticed that his hands were shaking slightly. He unlocked the door, helped her in, and walked quickly around to the driver's side.

"So much for public involvement," Eric said shakily, pulling himself in behind the wheel. In a second, his low-slung Jaguar sedan was slipping powerfully out of the back parking lot and into the Springfield traffic. Courtney felt his hand on hers. To her amazement, Eric seemed as rattled as she was. She gripped his hand back in a show of solidarity. It was a strange and powerful moment. Here she was with a world class financial wizard— trying to do the right thing. The fair thing. Even though no one understood.

"You knew all along what would happen, didn't you?" Courtney said quietly, breathing in the comforting new-car smell of the sports car, with its leather seats and high-tech dashboard.

"It wasn't so hard to predict," Eric replied, shrugging. His angular face looked worn, but handsome as ever in the oncoming headlights. "People will jump when they're treated unfairly. But they also jump when everything's fair and completely justified. They automatically think you have something up your sleeve."

Courtney looked down at her hand. Eric was still holding it. In a single, subtle move, she slipped it away, pretending to get something out of her purse.

"Oh, God," Eric muttered, checking his watch.

"I've got a conference call in five minutes. Would you mind stopping by my place for a minute? It's right up this block. I'll drive you back to the sorority afterward."

"Not at all. But I really do have to get back soon. I've got a meeting in an hour and I haven't prepared for it."

Eric swung the Jaguar into a parking space before a stately home on the edge of the campus. Its many windows were trimmed with identical dark green shutters. The dimly lit front porch was painted red, and heavy brass knocker hung on the door. "It's a beautiful place," Eric said casually. "The Peabody Mansion. Nearly a century old and beautifully preserved. The university uses it for visiting dignitaries," he added with a chuckle. "But I guess they didn't have anyone dignified at the moment, because they let me use it for a few weeks."

Courtney let out a small laugh. "You're more important than any dignitary. You're saving the university from financial disaster."

Eric looked over at her and smiled. "I wouldn't be doing so well without my personal intern. Your research and ideas are invaluable. Now come on in."

Courtney looked up at the elegant mansion, bordered by a few charming guest cottages nestled in the trees. She hadn't felt so good about her life in a long while. And she hadn't admired anyone as much as she admired Eric Sutter.

"Okay," Courtney said as she got out of the car and followed Eric up the porch steps. "I could use a breather between meetings, anyway."

Eric unlocked the front door and led her into a beautifully decorated living room lined with antiques, books and two elaborate fireplaces. "Make yourself at home. I'll be back in a minute."

Courtney watched Eric leave the room and go up the staircase. Then she sat down on the couch and smiled to herself. The more she thought about her situation, the stronger and more independent she felt. It was as if she could see her career unfurling before her like a red carpet. Her life would be filled with last-minute meetings like this. She'd meet fascinating people. In-demand professionals who were tops in their fields.

She reminded herself that a career as a business-woman meant constant professional contact with men. She knew that meetings often dragged on into the evening hours and that she'd have to put up with some awkward situations to fit in.

But fit in she would. There was no stopping her now.

"Hi!" Courtney heard Eric pad back into the living room. She turned and saw that he had changed into a pair of jeans and a T-shirt. "My New Jersey client had to jump a flight to Chicago a few hours ago, so the conference call will have to wait." Courtney watched as he casually opened a paneled door, revealing a fully stocked wet bar. "Drink? Wine?"

"Uh, no thank you," Courtney said politely, silently wishing he didn't seem so relaxed. Only a few minutes ago, he'd been trembling like a little kid lost in a crowd.

"Oh, come on," Eric urged, pouring white wine into two balloon-shaped crystal wine glasses. He punched a button on the built-in stereo system. Soft jazz began to filter through the dim room. "After that crazy-people's convention, it's just what the doctor ordered."

"No, thanks," Courtney replied, stiffening as he sat down next to her on the couch. "Umm, about Saturday's athletic-department meeting. I've already made a few notes." She reached into her bag on the floor.

Eric stopped her with his hand. "I know we should talk about that, but I'm still a little on edge." He smiled at her. "Let's just unwind and forget work for a little while."

Courtney opened her mouth, but couldn't think of anything to say.

"I don't know," he continued easily, leaning subtly toward her. Courtney could practically smell his aftershave. "Bad situations like the one we just went through in the student union are just part of the job. The trick is knowing how to relax . In this business, you have to work hard, but you also have to know how to escape and play hard."

Courtney laughed nervously. "I guess that's the credo of a lot of business people."

"The most successful," Eric said as he swirled the wine in his glass. "I can see that you're still a little upset, Courtney. What do you do to relax in your free time?"

Courtney could feel a trickle of perspiration running down her spine. She suddenly stood up, picked up the wine glass from the coffee table and took a sip. Then she strolled toward a framed print on the wall, pretending to be interested in it. "I swim and play tennis to relax," she said shortly.

Out of the corner of her eye, Courtney could see that Eric was getting up from the couch and walking up behind her. She had to think. There was something unfamiliar about the way he was looking at her in the low light. Something that was making her increasingly uncomfortable.

"I play too," Eric murmured over her shoulder. "In fact, I've got a mean backhand. Maybe we could play sometime."

"That'd be great. But I should go now," Courtney said. "It's getting late."

"Nonsense. I think you should stay for a late dinner. I'll call a local gourmet shop and ask them to deliver a delicious treat for two. There's no better way to end a stressful day."

"Thanks, but I really have to run." Courtney checked her watch purposefully. "My sorority sisters are waiting for me." She wasn't sure whether Eric had just tried to make a pass at her, but she didn't want to insult him by making the wrong assumption. It would only cause tension for the rest of her important internship. He was her boss. It could only mean trouble. Plus, all she wanted in her life right now was work and more work. No new relationships.

"Tri Beta is only a few blocks away," Courtney said, setting down her wine glass and fixing her eyes on the door. "I can walk."

"Walk? I'll drive you," Eric said firmly.

"No, thanks." Courtney grabbed her bag and headed out. "The fresh air will be soothing. See you tomorrow." As quickly as possible, Courtney slipped out the front door and ducked down the quiet street.

"Something happened back there," Courtney muttered to herself. "Or is it just my imagination? Am I being uptight, or am I just playing it smart?"

Five

> "Hi folks, this is K–R–U–S, stereo FM in Springfield. Ninety-point-five on your dial. Cody Wainwright, your host tonight for an evening of blowout country tunes and more."

KC tiptoed in through the door of the station early Wednesday evening, a brown paper bag full of dining-commons doughnuts in one hand, her briefcase in another. She smiled when she saw Cody's face under a red on-air sign behind the booth's soundproof glass.

KC looked around. KRUS's outer waiting room was furnished with orange crates, old car seats, stacks of yellowing newspapers, and cluttered bulletin boards.

Through the glass, KC could see Cody motioning toward the door. She tiptoed in and sat carefully down on a folding chair. She crossed her legs under her straight skirt, trying not to crackle the paper bag. The station's inner studio was even more chaotic, with its shelves of CDs and tapes, log books, ashtrays, empty soda cans, and beat-up scripts.

"On Friday night, we'll have excitement over on McClaren Plaza," Cody continued. "That's right, folks. The U of S will be hosting a live cable-television broadcast of the winners of the national *Laugh . . . Or Else* contest. Eight o'clock in the beautiful five-million-dollar Patchen Auditorium. Thanks, Mr. Patchen."

Cody was peeking into the bag and giving KC an okay sign with his hand.

KC stared at him. She'd been seeing Cody for the last week, but she still couldn't decide how she really felt about him. When her boyfriend, Peter Dvorsky, had left for Italy a while ago, she'd been totally convinced that she would never even look at anyone else again.

But Peter's letters didn't come as often as they used to. And he was usually out when she tried to call his *pensione*.

"Also comin' up this week—budget talks on the future of U of S athletic programs. I'm tellin' you, if you're a jock, and you want to find out what's goin' on, check out the Eric Sutter meeting in the student-union building at two P.M. this Saturday."

Cody carefully removed his mike from the stand. Then he turned toward KC in his swivel stool as he continued his announcements. She glanced at the silver band around his forearm. His long legs were crossed.

Being on the air, live, before a listening audience of thirty thousand people didn't seem to faze him a bit. In fact, KC thought she'd never seen an expression of such stillness—such calm. Maybe that was why she was so drawn to him. Cody was like a drink of cool, calm water after a long, bad spell of pain and loss.

KC began to relax in her chair, enjoying Cody's deep, twangy voice. She stared at his tawny face and the way his smooth, dark brown hair was shining under the light. His large eyes were the color of dark caramels—deep and so mysterious it made her wish she could sink into them.

"This next set is dedicated to all you confused lovers out there. You know who you are. It's a Springsteen set that's gonna *speak* to you."

KC looked up and saw that Cody was giving her a subtle wink. An arrow of pure warmth shot through her body as he slowly reached out and gave her hand the slightest touch. Then Cody reached back and punched a button that started the music. "It's not easy figuring out how you feel about someone—or what to do when you finally know," Cody added into the mike. "I just hope we can all get through it in one piece. Remember folks: Stay honest." He slowly turned up the volume and slid his stool closer to KC.

KC's heart was in her throat. She sat silently as he planted his hands on each arm of her chair, leaned forward, and kissed her. It was a gentle, warm kiss.

"Hi," KC murmured, staring into his eyes.

"Hi, KC," Cody whispered back. He kissed her again, this time a little longer. "You look very beautiful today."

"Oh, God," KC said drowsily, resting her forehead against his. "I don't know what to think anymore."

Cody slid back a little. "Think about what?"

"Us."

"Oh, well, let's see now. You've come to visit me. You've brought me greasy doughnuts. You've kissed me in a way that I don't remember ever being kissed . . ."

A smile sneaked out of the corner of KC's mouth. "What do you mean?"

Cody shrugged. "It was just different. It was very—soft."

KC leaned over and tickled his ear. What was it about Cody that made her want to break down her tough, all-business exterior? She'd worked for years to build it up. But now she couldn't seem to remember why. "It was a nice kiss," she agreed.

"And I think it says a lot about how you feel about me. But you're not ready to accept it."

"Oh, I see," KC began teasingly. "Inside, I'm just dying for you. But I haven't *accepted* it. Give me a break."

Cody straightened up and folded his arms across his brown leather vest. "That's right. You're fighting your true feelings."

KC's thoughts were jumbled. She knew that he was right, but she was too afraid to bring up the reason. "I wouldn't be so sure."

"Well, I am," Cody said in a steady voice. "You're not being honest with yourself. And it's because of Peter Dvorsky." KC squirmed in her seat. "What's the story with him?"

"Uh . . ."

"Are you committed to Peter? Are you in love with him? Or are you just using him to protect yourself?"

"What do you mean?"

"I mean that if Peter is going to be a barrier between us, I want to know. And I'd rather it be sooner than later."

KC slumped back down into the lumpy chair and stared into space. She was still trying to get used to Cody's directness. What was she supposed to say when she didn't even know how she felt? In the beginning, Cody had been more like a pleasant distraction than a serious date. It hadn't been easy losing her father to cancer right after Peter left. She'd fallen briefly into drugs and alcohol. Then meeting her natural mother for the first time had been an emotional roller coaster ride. Cody's straightforward attentions seemed like a peaceful refuge in her mixed-up life.

"KC?"

"Okay," she began shakily. "Well, I'm not sure about Peter. I talked to him a couple of weeks ago . . . but nothing's the same. I know that I was in love with him. But I'm not sure how I feel anymore."

Cody nodded. "Now we're getting somewhere."

"Sometimes I feel as if I'm talking to a stranger on the other end of the line," KC's words began to spill out as she realized how much she wanted to talk about it.

"It must be hard."

KC felt something clutch in her throat. "I just wish Peter would tell me he's seeing someone else. I mean he *acts* like he is. And then—and then . . ." she broke off.

"Then you'd be off the hook," Cody finished her sentence gently. He reached out and slowly wound a strand of her dark hair around his finger. "You'd have permission to see someone else too. Right?"

KC looked down at the worn carpet and shook her head. Her eyes were wet. What right did Cody have to read her mind, anyway?

"Look, KC," Cody's voice was gathering strength. "I don't know about you and Peter. But I do know what I need. And I need to know where I stand. I need the truth. Call him. Ask him how he feels."

"What?"

"What have you got to lose?" Cody urged her, suddenly picking up the station phone. His hand was poised over the buttons. "What's his number? Call him right now and ask."

KC grabbed the phone and slammed it down. "I can't."

"Okay, then," Cody challenged her. "Come over to my place later. It's a private guest cottage right next to the Peabody Mansion. You can call him from there. I'll pay for the call."

KC forced a smile. "Oh, I see. You just want to eavesdrop on us. You want to hear what I sound like when I'm talking with someone I'm crazy about."

Cody shrugged and turned away, looking up at the studio clock and checking his CD program. "Thirty seconds and I'm back on the air." There was a pause and KC stood awkwardly in the middle of the room, not knowing whether to stay or leave.

"Cody?"

"Just go, KC," he replied, adjusting a knob and straightening himself in his seat. "If you want to keep seeing me, you're going to have to make that call. We both need to know exactly where things stand."

"Okay, Liza, great monologue," a production assistant from the cable TV company shouted. "You're on a roll. I've never heard anyone have such hilarious problems."

"No one has problems like mine, hon," Liza cracked. "I have them flown in fresh daily from my parents' home in Brooklyn."

"Right. Right," the guy laughed. "Now, the way we'll start is—after the music, the stage manager will give you the nod, and you just enter from off left."

Liza released a brilliant smile and stared out at the nearly empty auditorium. She felt like a star already. "Sounds good to me."

"Yeah, and hold it there for just a minute please, Liza."

It was early Thursday morning. Liza had been called in to do a dry run of her comedy act to prepare for the next night's live television broadcast. Most of the eleven other winners of the national *Laugh . . . Or Else* contest had already arrived from universities throughout the country. A crew of technicians was setting up a row of enormous television lights close to the stage.

Liza glanced around and breathed in the wonderful dusty-oily smell of the place. She fluffed her mound of red hair and took another quick look at her outfit—a skintight, red sequined tank top over a pair of jet-black leggings. A pair of red high-heeled sandals completed the look.

"I've got the world on a string—sittin' on a

rainbow," Liza burst spontaneously into song.

There was a loud switching sound and the stage was suddenly flooded with intensely bright light.

"Yowie-zowie," Liza cracked, shielding her eyes from the glare. "How am I supposed to see my adoring fans with that monster lightbulb in my face?"

"That's television, Liza," the production guy called out. "Okay, we're going to want a down-light spot," he shouted to the crew. "Yeah. No. Okay. Iris it down to a four-foot diameter."

Liza shifted her position on the stool and fluttered her tank top. "You're gonna give me heat-stroke. Come on. I know I'm your first guinea pig, but give me a break!"

The television lights went down with a loud bonk and Liza could instantly see the profile of a familiar, curly head of hair in the back of the theater. *"Rich!"*

"Uh. Okay, I guess you're done for now, Liza."

"Thanks," Liza sang out, running off stage and ducking out the side door that led into the theater. In a few moments, she had run breathlessly up the aisle and was in the arms of her boyfriend. "How did you like it, Rich? Was I awesome or what?"

She watched Rich look down at her curiously, then give her a smile. His arm was snaking slowly around her waist. "You were brilliant, Liza. No one's going to believe this is your first comedy act. You're a pro."

Liza gazed at his cuddly face, pinched his cheek, and kissed him. It was incredible. From the Hollywood biographies she'd read, it was really unusual for a star to find personal happiness when their career was hot. The two almost never went hand in hand.

A pang of regret gripped her for a moment. If only things hadn't happened the way they did at the U of S's comedy contest. The day that Rich had been scheduled to compete against her with his amazing ventriloquist act, Liza had hidden his dummy backstage. He'd been forced to drop out. If it hadn't been for her moment of total, irrational thought, Rich might have been rehearsing for a television appearance, instead of her.

The amazing part about it was that Rich had found out—and had actually forgiven her. The only thing left for her to do was commit herself to a totally honest show-business life. Never again would she ever screw someone over.

Rich took her hand and led her to the back row of seats, where they sat down together. "I just got a letter from my dad," he said, pulling an envelope out of his back pocket.

"Really?" Liza curled up happily next to him. "And what does your fabulous television-producer father say?"

"Well, actually, it's pretty incredible," Rich said quietly. "He wrote me about a new pilot he's producing called *Greasy Spoon*. It's about a New Jersey diner where—"

Liza laughed. "A New Jersey diner? I've been to a zillion of those dumps."

Rich nodded. "Yeah, well, the thing is—he's looking for a teenage actress to play the role of Red. You know, sort of a wise-cracking, flamboyant waitress-type."

Liza's eyes widened.

"Dad wants to use a new face for the show, but he hasn't been able to cast anyone," Rich said calmly. "He asked me to keep an eye out on campus."

A bolt of sheer bliss surged through Liza. "Rich—you don't think—you don't mean—"

Rich smiled down at her.

"Are—are you kidding," she exclaimed, grabbing the letter out of Rich's hand. She stared at the letterhead on the stationery. "Bernard Greenberg Productions, Inc., 10098 Taylor Street, Hollywood, California."

"Would you like me to mention your act to him?" Rich asked innocently. "Maybe he could catch the Friday show on television."

"Oh, Rich, thank you," Liza screamed, throwing her arms around his neck and kissing him over and over. *"Thank you thank you thank you. I'll love you forever for this. Absolutely Forever!"*

Liza planted a final, deep kiss on Rich's mouth. And although the kiss he gave her back wasn't quite as strong, she knew it was just because her adorable, wonderful boyfriend was a little bit shy.

"I'm the luckiest person on the face of the earth," she whispered. "And I don't really deserve it at all."

"Oh, you do," Rich said. "You do."

Six

Courtney took a sip of her frothy cappuccino and watched KC set up neat piles of notes and seating arrangements on the hand-hewn bench table. It was Thursday morning, and they were in Springfield's funky off-campus coffeehouse, The Beanery.

"Bon Appetit will cater a light buffet for seventy-five guests at seven fifty a head, including refreshments," KC was droning efficiently.

Courtney's lids were beginning to droop with exhaustion, but breakfast was the only time she and KC had free to discuss the next day's big alumni function. Now she was glad that KC had chosen a coffeehouse for their meeting. Coffee was the only thing that would get her through the day.

"Good," Courtney managed, taking another gulp of caffeine and biting into The Beanery's experimental whole-wheat-broccoli-cheese quiche.

After her confusing encounter with Eric in the Peabody house the evening before, Courtney had spent the rest of the night tossing in her sleep. She couldn't stop wondering what had happened. Was it her imagination, or had Eric actually been attracted to her? It certainly seemed as if he had been. So, was she right to leave his house so quickly? Should she have stayed to talk it over with him?

"Courtney?" KC was saying.

"Yes?"

"Courtney, this is important," KC reminded her. "Tomorrow night we're going to have seventy-five heavy-duty Tri Beta alums for dinner. It's got to be just right."

"Sorry, KC." Courtney straightened up. "Go ahead."

"We're going to break bread with the Honorable Angelica Bradford," KC went on, her eyes shining with excitement. "That's just the sort of connection you need, Courtney."

Courtney nodded. "Former Ambassador to the Netherlands," she recited. "United Nations official in charge of European environmental affairs. Anyone wanting to get into international relations—like me—would die to meet her. And she knows my parents."

"No!"

"She's an old friend from their days at Princeton."

"Perfect," KC said, stunned. "So get out there and impress her. If you don't, I will. I'll tell her all about your Eric Sutter internship and your other amazing accomplishments."

Courtney smiled, grateful for KC's upbeat mood. After all KC's recent troubles, she was doing better than ever. It was almost as if the tables had been turned. Maybe it was time for Courtney to lean on *KC* for a change.

"KC?" Courtney began shyly, fiddling with her cappuccino cup. Perhaps KC would understand her dilemma with Eric. She'd been in the working world for several years now, and knew what it was like to deal with men on the job.

"Yeah?" KC mumbled, starting another list.

"Um—have you ever been in a situation with a guy where you thought things were really—you know—serious and professional . . ."

KC was nodding absently as she jotted something down.

"But then you start thinking it's more than that . . . ?"

KC's eyebrows shot up. "Of course. It's impossible to figure guys out. Take Peter. First he acts like he's all business when I modeled for the Classic Calendar shots. Remember when he took those pictures? Then it turns out he really likes me. Then he denies it. Then we get together. Then he leaves for Italy, pledging his love to me. Then he acts distant on the phone, as if he were involved with someone else. It's absolutely impossible to figure out."

"But . . ."

"Think of the book we could write if we could decipher the male animal. Think of the hundreds of thousands in royalties. Millions of women are trying to figure men out. They'd be dying for this information."

"Yes, but . . ."

"Even if I *did* decide someday to call Peter up on the phone and tell him I wanted to see—oh, Cody Wainwright for instance," KC went on. "Peter would probably say, 'Sure. Okay. No problem.' When in *reality* he might be totally heartbroken. There's just no way of actually knowing."

"Right," Courtney agreed, deciding it wasn't the right time to talk to KC about Eric. They were too busy planning the alumni event, and KC was obviously preoccupied with her own problems. Besides, Courtney didn't know if she even had a problem.

"Okay." KC flipped her notebook shut and began stacking sheets of paper. "We're done. The only thing left is the decorations, which Diane is organizing. And limo service from the airport, which I'm arranging. But if you can meet Ms. Bradford at the airport, that would be perfect, Courtney."

"I'll try." Courtney said absently, standing up and nearly knocking her head on a hanging plant. "I've got to run, KC. Eric Sutter called a nine o'clock meeting over at his office."

"Knock him dead. I'll see you later."

"Uh, sure," Courtney said as she slipped out of the booth and wiggled her fingers in farewell.

When she stepped out on the sidewalk and headed toward campus, she could see that the early morning clouds had parted. The sweet scent of leafing cottonwoods was in the air. She breathed deeply, fully awake now, and her spirits lifted.

Taking brisk steps across the avenue, Courtney headed up a tree-lined path that lead to the

Administration Building, then branched off to Forsythe and Parker Halls. A guy on a skateboard sailed smoothly past her, and two girls from her sorority waved gaily from across the sunny field. It was a beautiful day. Nothing could spoil it.

In fact, the more Courtney thought about Eric, the more she was convinced the whole problem was in her head. Plus, even if he *had* been attracted to her last night in his living room, there wasn't any law against two mature adults putting the issue aside and buckling down to their work. After all, Eric was a highly educated grown man—preoccupied with a thousand financial details. He was a far cry from the fraternity guys she was used to, who were bent on proving themselves with the girls and thinking up clever come-ons.

Courtney sighed to herself and smiled. The whole thing was ridiculous. She didn't have anything to worry about.

Her mind clear of worry, she continued to Eric's office, where a few chairs were gathered in a half circle. The meeting was about to begin. Besides Trevor and Phillip, Eric had also given an internship to a heavy girl from the university's math department.

"Ah-ha," Eric welcomed Courtney from his casual perch on the edge of one of the intern's desks. He was wearing a perfectly cut blue suit, starched white shirt, red tie, and shiny wing-tip shoes, as if he were about to attend an important meeting. "Here she is. Join the group, Courtney."

Courtney smiled politely and sat down next to the other girl.

"Rosalyn has crunched some numbers for us on the athletic budget and has provided us with a statistical analysis of future revenues and expenses using a range of alternative measures," Eric began briskly. "I've distributed your report as well, Courtney, and I've asked Trevor and Phillip to do further research on a few items I've highlighted."

Courtney nodded and relaxed. She was feeling better about Eric already. He was cool, efficient, and all-business this morning. It was obvious that he'd noticed her discomfort last night, and had politely backed off from any hint of a personal relationship.

"The meeting on the athletic budget will be held Saturday at two o'clock in the gym," Eric continued. "Basically, my plan involves a fifteen-percent across-the-board cut of all athletic budgets through the rest of the fiscal year and into the next."

"Those guys are going to scream," Trevor spoke up. "Their budgets haven't been touched by human hands in a decade. They pride themselves on being big money-makers."

"They are big money-makers," Eric came back smoothly. "That's why a fifteen-percent cut for them is peanuts. Now, I want all of you present at the meeting. There may be some more detailed numbers I won't have at my fingertips. So I'll want you to be my fingertips. All stats and historical analysis available. Got it?"

The group nodded and murmured in agreement.

"If I need to see you before then, I'll let you know," Eric said. "Thanks for coming. Oh, Courtney? I need to speak to you for a moment about your part of the research, please."

Courtney nodded and followed him into the inner office, as the rest of the staff left through the door. Sitting primly on a chair near a filing cabinet, Courtney clasped her notebook in front of her and gave Eric a serious look as he closed the door.

She watched as he paced nervously across the carpet, his hands in his pockets. His ruggedly handsome face was bent down. He stopped and rested against the edge of his desk.

"This is going to be one hell of a bloodbath on Saturday," Eric said looking at Courtney seriously. "I didn't want to make too much of it with the others." He smiled. "Don't want to scare them off."

"I see," Courtney said firmly.

"There are going to be a lot of objections—even violent ones—from the athletes and coaches," he continued. "But I know my plan is right."

Courtney paused. A tiny thread of annoyance slipped through her. *His plan? Wasn't that my plan?* she thought. *Almost to the last detail?*

"It's the only fair thing to do," he continued. "And the regents are backing me up one hundred percent."

Courtney nodded. "Then you have nothing to worry about. The fifteen-percent across-the-board cuts are standard with the region's public universities this year." She cleared her throat. "Research has shown that athletic-department cuts do not substantially affect revenues, and that recovery is rapid when budget levels eventually increase."

"You're absolutely right." Eric smiled, his eyes intent on Courtney.

Courtney stood up. "Well, let me know if you need anything else." She started to head for the door.

"I *do* need something else," he replied, walking quickly to the doorway and casually stretching his arm across it.

Startled, Courtney backed up. Her face was

starting to get hot with embarrassment. "What is that?" she managed calmly.

"I need to know if you enjoy working for me," Eric asked with a teasing, almost pouty look. Then he lowered his face toward hers so that they were practically eye-to-eye. "I certainly enjoy working with you."

Courtney backed up some more. "Of course, I do. I like my job," she mumbled.

"Then why did you leave so abruptly last night?" he whispered teasingly. "You hurt my feelings."

"Your . . ." Courtney broke off, her eyes growing wide. She felt the edge of his desk bump up behind her, so that she was now pinned in place.

"Well," Eric said, moving casually forward, "I was just worried that you were still upset about the crazy scene at the student-union hearings. Pretty rough stuff," he murmured, lifting his hand up and stroking Courtney's cheek with the back of his hand.

"I wasn't upset," Courtney said quickly, her eyes darting toward the door. Quickly, she slipped over to the side, hoping to walk casually around Eric.

Instead, he caught her by the shoulder. "You must have known I was interested."

Courtney's mouth dropped open in horror. Her instincts *were* right. Her worst nightmare had come true.

"Come on," he persisted. "I've seen the way you look at me. The way you took this personal liaison job so quickly . . ."

"Wha . . . ?"

Eric's hand was slipping over her shoulder onto her back, so that he was pulling her closer. Courtney was paralyzed with confusion. "You wouldn't have come back with me to my house last night if you hadn't been attracted."

"You insisted," Courtney gasped. "You wanted to talk about the meeting."

Eric smiled. "Nice sorority girls like you don't do that kind of thing unless they know exactly what's going on. I know all about your world."

At that moment, Eric dropped his head slowly down onto her neck. "Don't play games. We don't have time. You knew what was involved when you took this job," he whispered.

"Stop it!" Courtney suddenly yelled. She saw movement in the outer office. "I have no idea what you're talking about. I took this job because I wanted the experience. The last thing on my mind was getting involved with you. What kind of a person do you think I am?"

"I love it." Eric moved toward her again. "You're so full of spirit. You're so beautiful. I know this is just part of your game."

"Get away!" Courtney said, as the phone rang. She watched as Eric stopped and gave her an irritated look. He straightened his tie and picked up the phone.

Trying desperately to control herself, Courtney sped out of the office, straightening her jacket and smoothing her hair. But just as she turned the corner toward the front desk, she stopped in horror. There, standing in the entryway was Dash, looking as scruffy as ever.

"What are you doing here?" Courtney demanded.

"Uh—I'm here to interview Rosalyn Meyers," Dash answered.

Courtney looked at him blankly.

"Your fellow intern," Dash said. "I'm a little bit late. Although it looks like everyone's conveniently gone."

"What does that mean?"

Dash smiled. "Uh, well, I just mean that you don't waste any time. One day you're madly pursuing me, and the next you've moved on to bigger fish."

Courtney glared at him. "You jerk. You know nothing."

"I know when I see two people necking," Dash shot back.

"Then maybe you need an eyesight test,"

Courtney snapped. "Things aren't always what they seem. But then you should know that. You are an investigative journalist, aren't you?" She sent Dash a deadly look and slammed the door behind her.

Seven

"What about the white satin number with the rhinestone belt, the one that's slit down to the naval?" Liza asked her roommate, Faith Crowley. Liza was staring intently at her chin in a compact mirror as Kimberly Dayton's van bumped its way toward a downtown Springfield shop.

Liza and Faith's neighbor, Kimberly, had offered to drive Liza downtown to pick out her outfit for tomorrow night's national cable TV broadcast. Lauren had come along for the ride.

Melissa was there too, only her mission was a different one. In a few minutes, Kimberly would be dropping her off at the Crisis Hotline Center to talk to Winnie.

Faith shook her head, smiling. "No way, Liza. You can't wear white on television. It puts glare on your face or something." She crossed her cowboy boots in the backseat next to Liza. "You're supposed to wear bold colors, like electric blue or vermillion red. Why are we shopping, anyway? All you have to do is wear the red sequined number you wore to the run-through."

Liza sighed and shook a pudgy finger at Faith's denim shirt and plain braid. "You may be a drama major, hon, but eye-stopping costume concepts aren't exactly up your alley. The red sequined is boring."

Lauren twisted around from the front seat. "Too boring?" she laughed, fluffing her hair off her face. "That outfit is about as boring as skydiving with Mel Gibson."

"Naked," Kimberly giggled, her long dancer's arms swinging the van into the downtown lanes.

"*Ahhhhggg!*" Lauren screamed.

"And if I'm going to be an authentic television star," Liza explained, barely controlling the joyful hysteria in her voice, "I have to stand out. I want my fans to say 'Oooh, did you see Liza Ruff? The beautiful redhead from *Greasy Spoon*? She wore the sexiest, most bizarre dress to the Emmy Awards. I want to be just like her,'" Liza finished with a sappy drawl, sending everyone but Melissa into convulsions.

Melissa glared at the group, then stared out the window. In a way, she wished she could jack her energy level up to theirs, but at the same time, everything they were talking about seemed so pointless. So futile.

Only a few weeks ago, the same group had driven downtown to fuss over *her*. And what had happened after all the fretting and squealing and thrilling over her wedding dress?

What happened is that I got dumped. I didn't need the wedding dress after all, Melissa thought bitterly. *The whole trip was a waste of everyone's time.*

She twisted a strand of her short red hair and gazed down at her battered sweatpants and faded U of S track T-shirt. *Who cares what Liza wears to the stupid show? Why are they all making such a fuss? It'll probably be a flop anyway, just like my wedding was.*

As Lauren and Faith batted one of Liza's large powder puffs back and forth, Melissa drummed her fingers nervously on the door handle. She wished Kimberly would hurry up so she could see Winnie. After all, Winnie had been her roommate and her first friend at the U of S when they were incoming freshmen last fall. Winnie, more than anyone, might be able to understand what had happened to her.

Maybe Winnie could tell her what people were supposed to do when they didn't want to do anything at all.

Still, Melissa remembered, it had taken her at least a week to get up the nerve to call Winnie for help. And another two days to actually decide to make the trip to the Center.

"Get aw—*ay*," Faith was giggling as Liza playfully tried to paint her with a tube of lipliner.

"Well," Kimberly began, "I have a theory. Liza wants to wear white because she's got something on her mind. Like Rich. You know: Goin' to the chapel and I'm gonna get marr—ied . . ."

There was a sudden silence.

Kimberly glanced back guiltily at Melissa. "Sorry."

Melissa felt a bolt of anger and frustration shoot through her. It was almost a relief. At least she was feeling something. "That's okay. Would you please stop the van and let me out here?"

"Sure," Kimberly said in a tiny voice, signaling right and pulling up to the busy sidewalk.

"Thanks," Melissa barked, sliding the side door

open, hopping out, and slamming it as loudly as she could.

Okay. Okay, Melissa thought as she got her bearings and checked the street signs. *I should be eternally grateful to Kimberly for not turning me in for all the stupid dorm thefts I pulled off. Especially when everyone thought she was the thief. But now she just gives me sorrowful looks and can't even talk to me. Plus, she never could keep her foot out of her mouth.*

Melissa shoved her hands into the pockets of her sweatpants and turned right off the main drag, down a row of small offices and shops.

"Everyone knows I'm in trouble, but no one wants to deal with me," Melissa muttered to herself, tears welling up in her eyes. "I'm invisible the way I am now. Everyone is still looking around for the old Melissa."

She checked the hotline's address on a slip of paper, then looked up at a freshly painted green door, bordered by two large windows on each side.

CRISIS HOTLINE. HELP WHEN YOU NEED IT, a sign read. Below, a box of red geraniums bobbed in the sun.

Taking a deep breath, Melissa opened the door and went in. She glanced nervously around the high-ceilinged room, lit harshly with rows of fluorescent lights, but softened by a few hanging plants dangling from the beams.

As Melissa walked cautiously into a waiting area, she could hear the faint sound of someone talking intently behind a makeshift acoustical divider. A few bright posters livened the bare walls, and a small sign propped up next to a bell read: RING FOR HELP.

Melissa rang the bell and flopped into a nearby folding chair. Soon, she could hear footsteps.

"Melissa!"

She looked up and pushed her stringy hair out of her eyes. But it wasn't Winnie. It was Josh.

"Hi, Josh," Melissa said wearily, not getting up. She crammed her hands deeper into her pockets. "I'm here to see Winnie."

"Oh," Josh said gently, sliding into the chair next to hers. "Uh. Did she ever return your call?"

"Nope," Melissa replied.

"Oh."

"But you told me she'd be here this afternoon, so here I am," Melissa continued, staring to wonder why she came in the first place. Looking at Josh only reminded her that he and Winnie were the ones who actually got married the day she was supposed to marry Brooks. Josh and Winnie had been smart. They'd simply slipped off and done it at an anonymous Nevada chapel. She and Brooks had been idiots—turning the day into a circus and making fools of themselves in front of the hundreds they'd invited.

"Is Winnie here?" Melissa demanded.

"Uh. No, she isn't," Josh said, shifting uncomfortably. "I'm sorry."

Melissa sighed. "So much for friends."

Josh reached out and touched her arm. "It's not you, Mel. Winnie's . . . Winnie just hasn't been herself lately. In fact, she's at home now, taking a nap."

Melissa gave him an exasperated look. "Josh, I lived with Winnie for many, many months. And she never once took a nap."

Josh nodded. "Yeah. I know. I'm a little worried about her." He ran a hand through his hair. "Listen, I'm sorry. Maybe you could wait for Teresa Gray. The only problem is she's got about five people on hold right now. I'm just here setting up a mailing list for the center on their computer. I'm not a trained counselor or anything . . ."

"Right, right," Melissa said softly, the empty hole inside of her growing. She wondered what being a trained counselor had to do with being a friend. Was Josh going to be like the rest of them? Was he just going to kick her out because he had no idea what to do with her? She breathed in. And when she breathed out again, a long, bitter sob poured out.

Melissa felt Josh's arm around her shoulders. "Melissa? Look. Talk to me. Winnie sometimes tells me I'm a total failure in the sensitivity department, but why not give it a shot?"

"I don't know," Melissa began wearily, leaning her forehead shakily into her fingers. When it came right down to it, she didn't know where to begin. How could she put into words what she barely understood herself?

"Are you getting back into your running?" Josh asked. "I know this sounds stupid. But—but you're such an incredible athlete. I mean, if I had your talent, I'd be out there pounding the track, getting my frustrations out . . ." He stopped just as his voice began to rise, and he flopped back in his chair. "But you're not me, are you? You're *you*."

"Yeah," Melissa agreed, a small ray of hope flickering through her. "I'm me. And I am back at practice. I'll lose my scholarship if I don't go, you know. But I don't have any concentration. And my energy level's in the dust. I just keep thinking about Brooks and wondering what happened."

"Have you talked to him?"

A bitter chuckle rose up out of Melissa's throat. "Are you kidding? He won't talk. All I have is a letter. And all he could say was that he couldn't go through with the wedding. He wouldn't even say why."

"Bummer."

Melissa sunk her head in her hands again. "I can't seem to shake this terrible feeling that nothing will ever be the same. I mean, how can you ever trust anyone? It all seems so useless and silly to get worked up about things the way I did before the wedding. Everything can blow up right in your face when you least expect it." She stared sadly at the toes of her running shoes. "How do you and Winnie do it? I mean, aren't you afraid?"

She looked up and saw that Josh was staring at her. His eyes were wide open, almost frightened, and his lips had parted a little. "Well, I don't know," he mumbled. "I guess we haven't gotten to that point yet."

"Sometimes I see Brooks on campus," Melissa rambled on, "and he looks right through me—as if I were invisible. For a while, I was so furious, that I—I actually went around taking cash out of purses and bags I'd find in the dorms." She stopped.

"Yeah. *I* was the dorm thief. Can you believe I've sunk so low?"

"I wish I knew how to help, Mel."

Melissa had started to clench her fists in anger. She was pounding them against the seat. "Sometimes I just wish I were sick. Really, really sick or something. Terminally ill. Then maybe Brooks would think about what he did. Then maybe he'd feel something. Maybe he'd talk to me."

"You need to talk to him, Melissa. And he needs to talk to you. It's the only way."

Melissa felt herself falling into Josh's hug. She was sobbing now, long and deep. It felt bad and good at the same time. Something inside told her it was good that she'd at least started to talk. "I've got to go."

"I'm going to talk to Winnie, if that's okay with you, Melissa," Josh said. "I'll make sure she calls you. In the meantime, you've got to promise me something."

"What?" she replied, sniffing.

"Don't stop running."

She shrugged. "Sure."

"And get over to that pow-wow the athletic honchos are holding Saturday morning," Josh urged her.

"Why?"

"Because you need to be there," Josh said simply. "You're one of our top athletes. Those budget slashers and bean counters notice when people care, and this meeting's supposed to get everyone organized. Get back into life, Mel. It's time to move on."

"I'll try," Melissa whispered, sighing and standing up. "Thanks. I think I'll walk back to campus. It'll feel good."

"Melissa?" Josh said as Melissa opened the door. He smiled as she turned around. Then he cupped his hands over his mouth. "Run," he whispered hoarsely, churning his fist in the air for encouragement.

"Hello?" Winnie's voice sounded far-off and weary on the other end of the line.

"Hi."

"Hi, Josh."

"What are you doing?"

"Uh—oh studying," Winnie was trying to sound upbeat, but Josh could tell she was still sleeping. The faint sound of rustling sheets in the background gave her away.

"Liar, liar, pants on fire."

"Yes, I am. No, I'm not."

"Still tired?"

"No," Winnie replied, her voice getting louder. "What's up?"

"I just talked to Melissa."

"Oh, God. I wasn't there. I'm a creep. She'll never forgive me."

Josh sat down in Winnie's office chair and swiveled lazily. Just the sound of Winnie's voice soothed him. He wasn't sure if he'd helped or hurt Melissa during their conversation minutes before. Now he wanted to talk it over. "She needs help."

"Yeah," Winnie agreed. "She crashed bad after that bungled wedding. How did she sound? Did she say anything that worries you?"

Josh had to think. "Well, she cried. But she also talked. Let off some steam. I told her you were going to call her and that she needed to stick with the running."

"Good."

"And I had another idea," Josh added. He stopped swiveling and leaned his elbows on the desk. "I think she needs to have it out with Brooks. She's really bitter and confused. Can you believe that they've never actually talked about what happened?"

"No."

"I told her to go to that athletic-department budget meeting on Saturday. Brooks is bound to go too, if I drag him there. It might be a good way to break the ice. Maybe he can talk her into getting some counseling."

"Perfect."

"Win?"

"Yep?"

"Let's meet in a couple of hours at the Zero Bagel," Josh suggested. "We'll eat Terrible Goulash and have some fun. Maybe that'll perk you up."

"I'm not really up for it, Josh. I'm sorry."

"Well, then, Win, you're due for a checkup at the health center," Josh insisted. "You're not feeling well and I'm going to take charge."

"I'm allergic to doctors," Winnie complained. "They make me break out and have anxiety attacks. I'm just tired. I live a busy life and things have just caught up with me. Now I'm going to hang up. Okay?"

"Bye," Josh whispered. He placed the receiver down and sat back, rocking in the quiet office. Winnie's office walls were plastered with Polaroid pictures of her with Faith, KC, Lauren, Kimberly, and a half a dozen other friends she'd made on campus. Loops of hot-pink bunting hung over the office divider, and a huge stuffed kangaroo was propped up in the corner.

He hated to think of Winnie sick. It was ironic. Winnie's life was full of love, companionship, and interesting work. But she was stuck in bed. Melissa's life, on the other hand, was so frustrating she was actually wishing she were sick—even fatally sick—so that she could get attention. And *she* was perfectly well.

Josh suddenly stopped rocking the chair. He froze. A dart of pure terror ran through his heart. What if Winnie were seriously ill?

He stood up and began pacing back and forth, trying to remember how long Winnie had been tired and suffering from dizzy spells. Winnie had never been tired before for no reason. Everyone knew that Winnie was overflowing with boundless energy. She could run five miles and keep up a steady flow of commentary without losing her breath for a second. She could pull an all-nighter, ace the next morning's exam, and boogie through the rest of the day as if nothing had happened. She thrived on junk food, noise, and constant motion.

"I have to get her to a doctor," Josh mumbled. What if she were suffering from some terrible disease? Symptoms like hers could mean a lot of things. A lot of awful things.

Nothing can happen to Winnie, Josh told himself, slinging his green army-surplus book bag over his shoulder and heading out of the office. He flung open the door to the street and felt the warm afternoon breeze on his face.

I love Winnie. I love her more than I ever thought I could love anyone. If anything ever happened to her, I would die.

Eight

*L*auren's arms were like steel propellers as she churned toward the end of the university's indoor pool. It was late Thursday night and she was the only swimmer left in the cavernous facility. Her muscles were burning and she could barely suck enough air into her lungs, but she didn't care.

Twenty laps down. Twenty to go.

"Ugh!" she grunted, bending her knees and pushing off again with all her might. Her body was a strong instrument over which she had total control.

Fat, depressed, vulnerable Lauren was gone forever. In her place was a tough, lean woman who would never let herself get burned again. Dash, fake track-star Dimitri Costigan-Broder, Courtney, her parents, Melissa. They'd all worked hard to break her down and take advantage of her accommodating personality. But now it was over. She had kissed them good-*bye*.

All she wanted as she stared through her goggles at the dark painted lines at the bottom of the pool was to continue her steady regimen of writing all morning, swimming every night, classes, and work for the *Weekly Journal*. She could hardly wait for her self-defense class to begin in a few days.

As she turned her head for a breath, Lauren noticed a dark figure on the side of the pool. Ignoring it, she continued to knife through the water. Then, out of nowhere, a mass of swirling bubbles blurred her vision. She lifted her head up. Someone had either jumped or fallen in.

Lauren treaded water and whipped off her goggles. She stared angrily at a bare-chested guy with dripping dark hair, who was floating next to her. She squinted.

It was Dash.

"What the hell do you think you're doing?" she demanded.

"I couldn't get your attention," Dash answered,

his sopping red bandanna dropping slowly over his eyes. He pushed it up.

"You're still wearing your pants and shoes," Lauren said curtly, her voice echoing. "And here comes the lifeguard. This is just great."

Dash looked at the approaching lifeguard. "It's cool," he said. "I just wanted a chlorine bath."

The lifeguard nodded with a smile. "Girl trouble is one thing I understand," he said with a wink.

Lauren was furious. She pushed off again. A few seconds later, she felt hands grab her by the feet. Dash's strong arms encircled her and lifted her up out of the water.

"Dash!"

"We need to talk."

"I'm working out," Lauren insisted, wriggling in his grasp. "What are you doing?"

"Trying to get your attention," Dash answered. She stopped, dropped her feet to the pool's bottom, and looked at him. His face was shiny and dripping. His arms were still around her, so that his bare chest was pressed against her nearly naked body. There was a strange, quiet look in his eyes. "I've been standing at the edge of the pool waving my arms and yelling for the last five minutes."

"Couldn't you wait?" Lauren asked, trying to ignore the slippery sensation of his upper body against her skimpy racing suit. She tried again to wriggle away, then gave up.

A smile sneaked out of the corner of Dash's mouth. "You looked like a maniac out there." Slowly, he dragged a finger down the side of her dripping cheek. "What are you doing? Swimming a lap for every injustice in the world?"

Sensing that his muscles had relaxed for an instant, Lauren slipped quickly out of his arms and swam away from him as fast as she could. She could hear the hollow thumping sound of him swimming after her, and when she reached the other end of the pool, he grabbed her around the waist.

"Dash!" She gasped for breath. She was having a hard time concentrating on what she wanted to say. The smooth feel of his olive skin and the familiar curve of his back was starting to soften her. She could feel him twisting her wet body around so that she was facing him in the lukewarm water. His face drew near and his lips touched hers. Then, slowly and sweetly, he kissed her. Her head felt wobbly. Her feet bobbed up and down on the pool's bottom. Every curve in her body seemed to melt into his skin until the two of them became one slow-moving, slippery, underwater mass.

"It's no use," Dash said, finally coming up for air. He was breathing hard.

"What's no use?" Lauren's lips were nearly numb from his kiss. She took a cautious look into his dark eyes and immediately dropped it. It was too scary to see Dash this close. She was starting to understand how strong her feelings were, as much as she wanted to push them down forever.

"I don't want to be away from you anymore," Dash said, his voice quavering, almost desperate. Lauren had never heard tough-guy Dash talk like this. Something had happened. Again, she lifted her eyes. She could see now that Dash's lips were pursed tightly, as if the words had started an avalanche inside of him that he was trying desperately to hold back.

Slowly, she swirled the blue water with a free hand. "I'm not the same person anymore," she said cautiously. "You don't know me."

"I don't care," Dash insisted, gripping her tighter. "We'll start all over again. Just tell me what you want."

Lauren froze. She looked up at his pleading face and felt a rush of confidence. Dash wanted *her* to tell *him* what she wanted? In all the months they'd been together, it seemed like he'd always been the one to charge ahead, and she'd always meekly followed. Not once had Dash asked her what she wanted. She was staggered.

"Look, can't we just get back together?" Dash blurted. He released Lauren and spread his arms along the side of the pool. "I want that more than anything."

"Just like that?"

"Yes. I was crazy to let you go. I've been out with a few girls since we broke up, but they mean nothing. You're the only one I want."

Lauren bristled. "*You* let *me* go? Did it ever occur to you that it might have been the other way around?"

"Well, yeah, but . . ."

"And I'm the one you *want*? " Lauren continued, her anger rising. "Who do you think I am? Some kind of cave woman you can drag off by the hair simply because you've decided you *want*?"

Dash shook his head sadly. "No, Lauren."

Lauren drew herself up onto the side of the pool and kicked the water lightly with her toe. She remembered the miserable and humiliating moment weeks ago when she witnessed Dash and Courtney embracing on the Tri Beta terrace. Then she looked down at Dash bobbing in the water. "I don't know you anymore."

"What do you mean?" His eyes opened wide. "You know me better than anyone else."

She sighed, exasperated, slapping one hand against the wet concrete. "Courtney Conner?" she blazed. "Courtney *Conner*? What could you have been thinking? She represents everything we've ever worked against."

"I know."

"The cruel snobbery," Lauren ranted. "The mindless uniformity. The absolute ignorance of what's good and decent in people who don't have the means to join their exclusive club. How could you?"

"It's over. And I can explain."

"I don't want you to explain," Lauren said in a rush, energized by a strange new feeling of power. "I want you to *show* me how you feel."

"Okay. Anything. I'll do anything."

"Fine. Maybe I am interested in getting back together," Lauren admitted. "But you have to prove to me that Courtney is out of your system forever."

"Sure."

"I can't afford to go through hell again," Lauren declared. "I've come too far to let it all slip away. Especially over someone like that."

Dash was nodding his head in agreement. His

eyes were wide open—almost stunned, as if he had new respect for her. "Okay. Deal. I'm not quite sure what I can do to prove it to you, Lauren. But I will."

At midnight, that same night, KC was alone in her single room in Langston House. Slowly, she typed the last line of her ten-page report on small-business risk factors. Then she ripped the last page out of the ancient machine.

She stared wearily at the finished stack of work, stood up, stretched, and retied her bathrobe. The dorm seemed deserted. The only sound in the hall was the occasional humming of the soda machine near the stairwell. She walked over to the window and stared at the dimly lit paths that crisscrossed the dorm green.

It had been two weeks since she'd last talked to Peter on the telephone. His last letter had come nearly three weeks ago.

Three weeks.

A mere blip on the screen of life, right? KC asked herself. She closed her eyes and made herself remember his face. The feel of his back. The way he always cocked his head a little when he smiled at her. His soft brown hair . . .

KC twisted a strand of her own long, dark hair, then stopped. She hopped up onto the ledge in front of her window and drew her knees up to her chin. Peter's hair. Parted. But on the left or the right? She felt a nervous fluttering in her stomach. His camera bag. He always had a button pinned to it. But what did it say? *Just give me some focus?* Or was it *Just give me some flash?*

She covered her face with her hands. Three weeks wasn't a blip. It was an eternity.

Desperately, KC tried to think back to the last few moments she had spent with Peter in the Springfield Airport. It seemed they had spent most of their time holding each other and talking about the good times they had had together. They had even pledged themselves to each other, but . . .

KC shook her head in frustration. She remembered what Cody had said two days before in the KRUS studio.

If you want to keep seeing me, KC, you're going to have to make that call. We both need to know exactly where things stand.

"But how do you ever know where you stand?" KC said softly to herself. "Things change so quickly. Look at me and Peter. Look at Melissa and Brooks. Lauren and Dash. Nothing ever seems to stay the same."

KC looked at her watch. Just past midnight. That meant it was around eight A.M. in Italy. She knew she had to call him while she still had the courage. It was early there and she'd probably wake him, but it was now or never, she told herself. Cody was right. He needed to know where things stood.

Just then, KC realized that she needed to know too.

Grabbing her purse, KC tiptoed down the dreary dorm hall. It was dark, and light shone out in slivers from only one or two of the rooms. When she reached the wall pay phone, she dialed the familiar long series of numbers to get to the international phone system. Then, with trembling fingers, she punched in Peter's number at the *pensione*. There was a wait, then a crackling sound, and then a dial tone.

Please be there, KC prayed. *Please don't let Peter's landlady answer. I can't understand her Italian. Please just let me talk to Peter.*

"*Buon giorno!*" she heard a girl's voice on the other end of the line.

KC froze. Her tiny address book tumbled to the floor, and her arm got tangled in the metal cord trying to pick it up. "Uh. Hello," KC practically yelled into the phone, hearing her voice echo back before she could start again. "I'm trying to reach Peter Dvorsky."

"He's not home yet," the faint voice replied gaily through the surges of static on the line. "He must still be over at Ursula's."

"Ursula's?" KC said without thinking.

"Yes. Any message to leave?"

KC barely heard the voice on the other end. She pulled the receiver away from her ear and stared at it. Her knees were starting to buckle.

Peter had never mentioned anyone named Ursula. Yet he was at her place at eight in the morning. Correction. *Still* at her place. There was only one possible explanation. Peter's involved—seriously—with someone else and hadn't breathed a word to KC about it

"Can I take a message for you?" the girl asked again. "Hello?"

Slowly, KC lifted the receiver to her ear. "No!" she spat into the phone. "There's no message. No message at all. Ever!" Then she slammed down the receiver and raced back down the hall.

Nine

....

"I read the article about you in *Newsweek* last month, Ms. Bradford," Stephanie Bridgemont was saying, ducking her shoulder expertly into the circle of freshly groomed Tri Betas.

The Friday evening reception for outstanding Tri Beta alums had begun half an hour before. The house was bristling with linen blazers, elegant floral arrangements, and tasteful silver trays laden with crudités and hors d'oeuvres.

"Please," Angelica Bradford said, extending her manicured hand, "call me Angelica. And you are?"

"Stephanie Bridgemont," she replied, smiling

eagerly and shaking the famous Tri Beta alumni's hand with adoration. "My parents are Jim and Nancy Bridgemont, from Denver."

"Ah." Angelica's foxlike face nodded in polite recognition. Her weighty gold necklace and stern navy suit gave her a no-nonsense air of authority. "I do know your father and mother from their fundraising work. How are they?" she asked smoothly. "I hope the real-estate business is booming."

Tri Betas Marcia Tabbert and Diane Woo hung on the edge of the circle, half listening to Angelica's story about playing tennis with a member of the British royal family—and half watching the door for Courtney.

Meanwhile, Courtney was outside on the patio, cradling a distraught KC in her arms. The soft evening air smelled of flowers. The sound of tinkling glasses and laughter floated out of the house. But KC was inconsolable.

"I can't believe it's over," KC wailed, curling up even tighter on the soft lounge chair. "How could Peter get so wrapped up in someone else—so—so *fast*?"

Courtney slipped a clean handkerchief out of her jacket pocket and dabbed KC's tearstained face. Since lunch, she'd been trying to help KC cope with the bad news about Peter. But it didn't seem to do any good. "I know, KC," she soothed. "I know it hurts."

Actually, Courtney thought, she knew how it felt very well. But even though she was familiar with the pain of relationships, she was still totally mystified by the strange dances that went on between men and women. She couldn't think of one single harmonious couple in her circle of friends. A shiver ran down her back as she thought of her confrontation with Eric the day before yesterday. Since then her doubts about men had been doubling by the second.

"I've been completely *betrayed*," KC burst out angrily, then resumed her weeping into the handkerchief. "I will never forgive him. And I won't ever see or speak to him again."

"Okay, okay," Courtney murmured helplessly, leaning against KC and rubbing her back.

"Courtney!" Diane whispered loudly, sticking her head out of the French door leading onto the patio. "You're really late. Everyone wants to know where you are."

She turned away as KC threw back her head and glared defiantly at the potted begonias, ignoring Diane. "But, hey, I've got a life to live too," KC declared. "Peter's just assuming that I'm going to sit here in Springfield like a nun while he carries on in Italy with some airhead named Ursula. But I'm not. In fact, right after I meet Angelica Bradford and a few other of the nation's elite, I'm going to go right over to Cody's place and *throw* myself at him."

"KC," Courtney protested absently. She was only half listening now. She knew she had to make an appearance soon at the reception. People were noticing her absence. If only she could calm her own jangled nerves.

KC stood up, blowing her nose with determination. "I'm going to get in there. I might as well start focusing on the world of business. At least it's something I can count on. "

Courtney barely controlled the urge to let out a bitter laugh. Didn't KC know that work could be an emotional minefield too? "All right," Courtney tried to sound enthusiastic. "Why don't you go up and borrow something to wear from my closet? The red sheath would be good. I'll be up in a minute."

When KC had gone, Courtney sank wearily back in her patio chair. The function was heating up inside and she was due in soon to toast the outstanding alums. Still, she needed a moment to straighten out her confused thoughts, which had been swinging back and forth crazily over the last couple of days.

She pressed her fingers to her forehead and tried to think. What in the world had she done to make Eric think she was interested in him? Over and over, she replayed the scenes in her mind. Had she seemed too eager—too excited, perhaps—when he offered her the internship?

Courtney shook her head in frustration. Was it her willingness to meet with him in the evening? Sure, they'd met two or three times after dinner the week before. But they were on a tight deadline to produce the regents' budget recommendation and arrange the student meeting.

Was it her body language?

Maybe it was something he misread in her eyes.

She heard the sound of footsteps crunching on the gravel driveway that ran up the side of the huge Tri Beta mansion. Courtney pushed her silky hair out of her eyes. She looked up and felt her heart sink into her shoes.

It was Eric Sutter.

"Hi there!" he said gaily, waving a file in the air and acting as if nothing had happened. He took off his dark sunglasses. "I didn't see you in front, so I thought I'd duck back here and try to catch you."

Courtney breathed in deeply and stood up.

Every nerve in her body was prickling with anger, but she was determined to hold her head high. "Hello."

Eric squinted at her hopefully, then dropped his shoulders in exaggerated defeat. "Look," he began, shaking his head. "I'm sorry. I know you're upset with me."

Courtney didn't respond. She didn't want to say anything until she knew where he stood.

"I came by to drop off the draft of the athletic-budget talking points," Eric said sheepishly. "Please. Take a look at it. It's important to me that you read it."

Courtney reached out her hand and took the folder. "Fine."

He put his hands in the pockets of his pressed slacks. "Look. I'm sorry I came on so strong the other day in the office. I—I just got a little carried away."

Courtney breathed a sigh of relief. She dropped her shoulders, suddenly realizing that she had been holding them taut. "Well, I . . ."

He held his hand out. "Truce?"

Gingerly, Courtney extended hers, too. "I don't know what to say," she began, slightly confused. "I guess I was a little taken aback. This internship has been very important to me."

"I'm glad you feel that way."

Courtney smiled cautiously. "Of course. I accept your apology. I know we can work together."

She shook his hand, then began to release it. Slowly a pang of fear began to sink through her.

Eric was still holding on.

Her heart in her throat, Courtney looked down at her hand, then up into his eyes. Gradually, he was tightening his grip and pulling her toward him. Her eyes widened in horror as she saw him wink, then cast his gaze down the length of her body.

"I *know* we can work together—on the job and off," he said in a low voice. "Especially now that I know your style. I get it. You want tidy talk during the day. But I bet you want just the opposite at night."

Courtney gasped and began to wrench her hand away, but he only held on more tightly.

"It sounds like a turn-on," Eric said, continuing to leer at her. "My proposal is this: Steak and oysters for dinner tonight at the Blue Whale, then back to my place for a little fun later on. And hey, attendance is mandatory for a passing grade."

With a final ounce of strength, Courtney ripped her hand out of his and fled to the Tri Beta house's side entrance. Fury pounding in every cell of her body, she ran past a group of sisters assembling stuffed mushrooms, then up the back staircase.

KC looked up sharply when Courtney burst through the door of her room and slammed it behind her. "Courtney! What's wrong?"

Courtney marched across the room, looked out the window, then marched back to the door. She jammed her hands into her pockets and paced. Then she sat down and dug her fingers into her hair. "Eric Sutter."

"God, Courtney. What happened?" KC hopped toward her, slipping on her black pump.

"He's got this idea that I'm interested in him personally," Courtney said in a rush. She stood up again and began aimlessly rearranging the papers on her desk. "He keeps taking me aside. Talking about how we should get together. You know."

KC's eyes had widened. "No."

"Yes. He's constantly grabbing me and propositioning me."

KC sank down on the bed and stared out the window. "He's harassing you. Sexually harassing you. I don't believe it."

Courtney felt hot tears behind her eyes. "KC. What am I going to do?"

KC looked down at the red dress and bit her lip.

"Judy Webster, in my business class, did a report on sexual harassment in the workplace. What you're supposed to do is file a written complaint to your superior or department head."

Nodding, Courtney sunk down in her desk chair. "Right," she muttered, her voice harsh with sarcasm. "Eric *is* my superior. That's the whole problem. He'd hit the roof if I complained to someone. And who knows what he'd do to my grade and my internship?"

"Yeah," KC agreed. "That's the problem."

Courtney thought. "Maybe I could sit down with him and tell him to stop."

"Angela's report said complaining about it makes harassers stop only about a third of the time. But it's better than trying to ignore him."

"I'm going to quit," Courtney said, bravely lifting her eyes. "I can't work with someone like that. It's the only option."

"But Courtney," KC argued, "that internship is so important. It could be career suicide."

Courtney stood up and made a haphazard attempt to smooth her hair. "I'm going downstairs," she said bitterly. "I've got to make an appearance. Life goes on. Doesn't it?"

By the time Courtney strode into the reception, her Tri Beta sisters were in high spirits and

Angelica Bradford was positioned in the center of the room, entertaining the group with an amusing tale about a barge trip down the Rhine.

"Courtney!" Angelica called out, raising her glass of sparkling punch in the air.

All heads in the room turned politely. Instinctively, Courtney straightened her back and raised her head high. A smile automatically formed on her face and her arm extended graciously, as if on cue. "Angelica. Please forgive me for being late. Something important came up."

"She's broken her own dress code, too," she heard Marcia Tabbert whisper loudly. "It's semi-formal and Courtney's still in her study clothes."

"Now, now," Angelica broke in, taking Courtney's hand and drawing her warmly into the group. "I happen to know a thing or two about this remarkable young lady."

Courtney's smiled faltered. Angelica's grip only reminded her of Eric's move on the back patio.

"Uh-uh," Angelica shook her finger. "No frowning. I'm not going to tell any embarrassing stories." She turned and winked at the group. "Like the one about the stunts you pulled on your parents when you were ten and thought you were Elizabeth Taylor in *National Velvet*."

Courtney regained her composure. There was an

amused tittering among the velvet headbands and swishing silks.

"No," Angelica continued. "What I do want to say, however, is I'm sure what all of you say about Courtney Conner. I've known her parents since my early days in the banking business. She's a remarkable person. She has the kind of intelligence and drive it takes to make it in the real world."

Courtney's heart sank.

"So when I heard about Courtney's internship with one of the country's top economists and financial experts," Angelica continued, "I knew that she hadn't changed a bit. Congratulations, Courtney. I know that your work with Eric Sutter will be an important milestone in your future career in international relations."

For a moment, Courtney thought she was going to be sick. But she breathed in deeply and regained her balance.

Angelica raised her glass of sparkling punch. "I have a few words of encouragement I'd like to share with all of you this evening," she went on. "But first, I'd like to make a toast to Courtney. Good luck. How you succeed with a brilliant man like Eric Sutter will be a good indication of how you'll fare in the world you are about to take on. And we all know you're going to have nothing but success."

"Hear, hear," a few of the sisters murmured, holding their glasses in the air.

Courtney bobbed her head up and down like a puppet.

If the real world is full of people like Eric Sutter, she thought, *then I'd just as soon stay here at the U of S for the rest of my life.*

But as she watched her sorority sisters' nodding heads and impressed looks, a horrible realization swept over her. There was no way she could quit her internship. No one would ever understand. Rumors would spread that she couldn't hack the job. Or that Eric had gotten rid of her. Her reputation for excellence and achievement would go down the tubes.

As she began mingling with the rest of the elegant crowd, Courtney knew she would have to stick it out with Eric. She didn't see any other choice.

Ten

....

Flashbulbs popped. Television cameras bobbed up and down on cranes. Patchen Auditorium was one huge mass of hysterical laughing, screaming, and applause.

Then the final bow came. All twelve *Laugh . . . Or Else* comedians filed out in front of the curtain.

Rich winced as Liza strutted across the bright stage, waving ecstatically. In her hot-pink sequined tank top, red miniskirt, and bright red hair, she looked more like a shiny piece of hard candy than a human being.

The roar was throbbing in his eardrums as he

continued his limp clap, staring thoughtfully at the stage.

"Aghhhhh!" The cheers and laughter were out of control now.

He saw why. Liza, jammed into the middle of the line, had found yet another way to stand out. Rich shook his head in amazement. Instead of facing the crowd, Liza had turned around so that her bows and overjoyed kisses were being thrown backstage to an imaginary audience. All anyone could see was her flailing arms and her wriggling, ample bottom.

Josh and Brooks were laughing too as they stood to applaud.

"She's amazing!" Josh exclaimed, digging his elbow into Rich.

"She sure is," Rich said quietly, watching Liza suddenly turn around, cover her mouth, and pretend to be totally embarrassed. A few people from the audience began throwing roses at her feet. After that, the other eleven comedians good-naturedly turned toward her and applauded.

"She actually made me want to *like* those girls in high school who used to make loudmouthed jokes for attention," Josh said.

"Uh-huh," Rich mumbled as the curtain dropped and the house lights began to go up. The aisles were suddenly mobbed with hundreds of gasping, giggling bodies trying to jam through the exits and into the spring night.

Rich's thoughts were spinning like an efficient machine as the three of them stayed in their seats and waited for the crowd to thin out. Nervously tapping his feet, Rich inwardly steeled himself. In just a few minutes, Step Two of his plan would be kicking in. All he needed now was to be cool and act like Liza's future was the most important thing in the world to him.

After all, Rich thought, smiling secretly to himself, *in a way, that's perfectly true*.

"Hey, you modest son-of-a-gun," Brooks leaned his curly blond head forward, looking at Rich. "You didn't have to restrain your applause just because she's your girl."

Rich shrugged and gave him an awkward grin, glancing around the empty theater as the television crews began removing their headphones and slapping each other in congratulation. The show's master of ceremonies—a washed-up comedian Rich remembered from his father's Beverly Hills parties—cracked open a beer and began joking with an attractive woman holding a clipboard.

In a few minutes, Rich would meet Liza backstage. Meanwhile, however, Brooks and Josh were deep in conversation.

"Look, buddy," Josh was saying to Brooks, "I talked with Melissa just yesterday and she's in bad shape."

"She's running," Brooks said, a guilty look spreading across his rugged features.

"Yeah," Josh said, almost accusingly, "but she's just doing it to save her scholarship. I'm not a counselor or anything, but she's depressed. Really depressed. She looks like hell, too. Saying some pretty scary things about her state of mind. Did you know that Melissa was the one who'd been stealing money from people in the dorm? She never got caught, but that's how weird it's getting."

Brooks sunk his head into his hands and shook it slowly. "That is bad," he moaned. "I didn't know."

"You're going to have to talk to her. Fast," Josh insisted.

"Yeah," Brooks was nodding, "Okay."

Josh leaned his elbows into his knees and gave Brooks a hard look. "I talked her into going to that meeting with the athletes tomorrow morning. Get there early and talk to her. You do owe her that much."

"I know. I should have done it as soon as I called off the wedding. It's just been really hard on me, too." Brooks slapped Josh on the back. "Thanks."

Josh looked over at Rich. "Well, go on. Talk to Liza. I'll give you a lift back on the bike when you're done," he said, pulling out what looked like a large medical textbook from his book bag and opening it on his lap. He began reading with concentration.

"Back in a few," Rich agreed, making his way out of the seats and down the aisle toward the backstage door. Then he steadied himself, like he always did before he began an act. Taking a deep breath, he strode backstage and found Liza in a dressing room, surrounded by fans and several of the other comedians.

"_Rich!_" she yelled, standing up and throwing her arms around him. Her stage makeup was still on, making her look like a perspiring, overstuffed clown. "Did you like my act? Did you? Could you believe the roses?"

Rich fixed a grin on his face and extended his hand. "Come on. Let's call my dad. I know he watched the show."

"_Ah!_" Liza let out a short, joyful scream. "I'm too nervous!" She took mincing steps in her stiletto heels as he dragged her to a backstage pay phone.

"Relax," Rich urged, digging through his pants pockets for his plastic calling card. "The act was perfect. He's probably jumping for joy down there in Beverly Hills. He's not going to have to do anymore work casting the *Greasy Spoon* lead."

"This is just too crazy," Liza said, pretending to protest as Rich began punching the phone number. Only it wasn't his father's. It was the number for the Beverly Hills Tri-Plex Theater. A number he'd dialed a thousand times in high school."

Rich obediently punched in his long-distance calling-card number as Liza squeezed his hand and nuzzled his neck.

"I'm getting a dial tone," Rich said with feigned excitement.

"Oooooh!" Liza panted.

"This is a recorded message from the Beverly Hill Tri-Plex Theaters . . ." Rich heard the recording begin.

"Dad?" Rich yelled excitedly into the droning. "It's Rich! Did you catch the show?"

"EEEEeeeeeeee!" Liza muffled a scream by clamping a hand over her mouth.

"Adults, seven dollars, children under ten, four

dollars," the anonymous, nasal-voiced man in the recording blared.

"You did?" Rich replied, nodding with interest as if his father were giving him a detailed reply. He looked up, smiled and nodded eagerly at Liza.

"What's he saying?" Liza hissed, trying to grab the receiver out of his hand.

Rich held on tighter, afraid that Liza might actually overpower him and hear the recorded message. "Uh-huh," he continued to agree. He turned to Liza and gave her the thumbs-up sign. "She was great, wasn't she?"

"*AHHHHHH!*" Liza screeched, making tiny little claps and jumping up and down. "Please let him say yes."

Rich clamped his hand over the receiver. "He went nuts over you," he whispered loudly. "Says you're perfect for *Greasy Spoon*."

At this point, Liza started to turn pale. She rested her body back against the side of the wall and put her hand on her heart. "This can't be happening. Dear Lord. He liked me. Your dad liked me."

" . . . is rated R, showing at three thirty, five forty-five, eight ten, and ten thirty-five. Sorry, no passes and no bargain matinees."

"Uh-huh," Rich began nodding again. "Okay, I'll ask her. She's right here."

Liza gasped, as if she'd seen a ghost. "What did he say?"

"He wants you to fly out next week for a screen test."

"Oh, my . . ." Liza lifted a white arm up and hung it over his shoulder.

"He can't pay to fly you down, because—you know, you're new to the b–business and don't have an agent or anything. It's against company policy. But he says if you can make it, he's sure you won't regret coming."

Liza's head jerked up and down. "Yes, yes, yes, *yes*," she hissed. "Tell him I'm coming. I'll scrape up my last dime. I'll rob social security checks from little old ladies in the street. I'll lie. I'll cheat. I'll steal . . . I'll do *anything*."

Rich smiled. "Yeah, Dad," he said into the phone. "She wants to come. Huh? Oh okay. Yeah, that'll be fine. You won't be disappointed."

"And parking is available on the north, east, and south sides of the building . . ."

Rich hung up the phone and was immediately overwhelmed by Liza's overpowering embrace. Suddenly, her mouth was pressed to his. Her ample arms were encircling his chest like a vise. "Thank you," she murmured into his ear, followed by a wet tug on the earlobe. She wriggled her fingers through his dark, curly hair and put her fore-finger on his lower lip. "I'll never forget this."

"Neither will I, Liza," Rich replied, pushing her away a little, feeling happier and more satisfied by the minute. His call had gone exactly according to plan. She'd taken the bait even better that he'd hoped. "Listen. I know you've got a celebration over at Luigi's, but I've got a paper to finish and only so many hours to do it. Josh is waiting to buzz me home."

"Okay," Liza said dreamily, stroking his cheek. "This has been an incredible night. Thanks again."

Rich smiled. "You did it all on your own, Liza. Dad's going to send you a letter, through me, detailing the arrangements," Rich explained. "It should be here in a couple of days."

"Okay, bye," Liza whispered. "Thanks."

Bye, Liza, Rich thought with delight as he slowly let go of her hand and left to join Josh. *Thanks for being such a great fool. Because I'm having the time of my life. Wait until you see the fake stationery. Wait until you actually get to L.A. and find out that my Dad has no idea who you are.*

It's almost enough to make up for the fact that it was you up there on stage tonight, instead of me.

* * *

"Whew," Cody whistled as he and Dash finally escaped through the swinging glass doors of Patchen Auditorium's lobby. "That Liza Ruff's one hunk of talent, but don't get me too close."

Dash nodded, squeezing past four girls who were giggling and repeating one of Liza's hilarious jokes. "Too close and she'll bite your head off."

"That's show biz," Cody drawled, pushing his long hair back off his shoulder. "You gotta be tough. And is she ever."

"Do you know something?" Dash wanted to know. He swung his bleach-stained denim jacket over his shoulder and cocked his head thoughtfully.

"The last time I saw her act, I caught her stealing a prop from the ventriloquist act," Cody chuckled. "Rich Greenberg's. It was just before comedy contest. She apparently wanted this guy out of her way."

"Oh, yeah," Dash nodded. "You called her on it—on the air."

Cody shrugged. "Some women are hard to figure."

"Like KC?"

"Yep," Cody replied, his long legs carrying him smoothly down the path that led off-campus. "I'm crazy about that girl. And I'm not even sure why. I think she's still with Dvorsky." He shook his head. "That's life in the fast lane. You never really do know what's going on."

Dash shrugged and dodged onto the grass as a group of bicyclists wearing night reflectors rushed past them. "Hey. I know what's going on as far as Lauren's concerned. I want her back. But that doesn't solve the problem."

"She goin' with someone else?" Cody wanted to know, pausing at the point where he turned off toward the Peabody Mansion guest houses. He rocked slowly on his heels, staring steadily at his friend.

"No," Dash said, punching the air with his fist. "She's just stuck on the fact that I went out with Courtney."

"Oh, yeah," Cody said with a knowing look. "The sorority president."

Dash shook his head. "Why I let myself fall into her clutches I will never know."

"Here's a wild guess," Cody replied. "She was beautiful and eager."

"I was a fool and she was a crazy person," Dash spat back, running his hand through his messy hair. "It was hell. One minute we were having a few dates. The next minute she was calling me at home at all hours. Leaving flowers at my door.

Bothering me at the *Journal*." Dash let out an exasperated laugh. "Then, after I finally tell her to stop, it's all over. She turns around and picks someone else up. Poor guy. I saw her just the other day in his office, just as wacko as ever."

"I hear you," Cody agreed. "I heard you two at that Rosebud Dance at the Tri Betas. She was real confused and upset after you left that night. And you weren't too pleasant yourself."

"Yeah, well, now she can get upset over Eric Sutter," Dash said bitterly. "*I'm* a free man."

"Sutter?" Cody's eyes shot up, as he turned to go.

"Yeah, can you believe it?" Dash called out over his shoulder. "Take it easy."

Cody fingered his silver Cherokee bracelet as he headed down the path toward his small cottage. Nestled around the stately Peabody Mansion, the houses were primo living situations that usually had a waiting list a mile long.

When he reached his place, he unlocked the door and immediately grabbed a rickety lawn chair from his tiny hall closet. All he wanted to do was sit in the cool evening air and stare at the stars for a few hours.

And think about KC.

Cody unfolded they chair and sat down. Then

he put his head back and stared up at the glittering sky. The evening was so clear and calm he knew he could have stretched his body out on the soft grass and fallen asleep, dreaming of the stars and KC's beautiful gray eyes. A noise made him lift his head up. He listened for a moment, then shook his head in frustration.

Loud laughter and conversation were pouring out of an open ground-floor window in the mansion. Quietly, Cody sat back and tried to ignore it. But once he realized it was probably Eric Sutter, he began thinking about Courtney. And within a few minutes, Cody's imagination was spinning. Who was she, really? Was she as crazy as Dash made her out to be? Could he really judge her based on the way she looked?

"Ha, ha, ha, ha," Cody could hear Eric laughing, probably on the phone, since he couldn't hear anyone else talking. "Yeah. It's working out fine, actually. No, flat fee. A pretty upfront, hands-off board. Yeah. Some blood ahead with the beefsticks in the sports departments, but hey. What else is new?"

There was a long silence. Cody leaned instinctively toward the window.

"Yeah. That too," Eric continued. "You bet I set up those internships. You don't think I'm actually going to do all the work, do you?" Pause. "Of course. Met a beautiful blond young thing. God. You should see her. A face that would knock your brains out. And legs. I'm in heaven. Yeah. Okay. Talk to you from Denver, then."

Cody felt slightly ill. Dash had been right about Courtney. She *was* a little crazy, getting mixed up with someone like Sutter, who sounded like he was just as much of a nutcase as she was.

But it wasn't his business, so Cody stretched his long legs out in front of him and flopped his head back again, nestling his hands deep in the pockets of his leather vest. Maybe he could forget everything for a few moments.

After several minutes, though, he smelled a familiar scent in the soft night air—sensed a familiar movement.

A pair of cool hands closed over his face. Cody felt silky hair brushing against his cheeks, then a slim and smooth body slipping into his lap. When the hands came off, he saw that it was KC, and she was bending her lips down to his.

"I called Peter," KC said, drawing her head slowly away from his so that he could see her gray eyes, her smooth skin, and the beautiful curve in her bottom lip. "I found out that he's seeing someone else. We agreed that we should both see other people."

Cody opened his mouth to protest. People didn't break emotional ties like that so easily. At least KC wouldn't. She wasn't that tough.

"Cody?" KC whispered in his ear. Her face was so close. Her eyes were so intense, and her delicate fingers were beginning to stroke his cheek. Every nerve and muscle in his body was melting into hers.

Thank you, Peter. Thank you, Cody found himself thinking as he pulled her closer. But when he felt her soft lips on his, everything in his brain came to a halt, and he wasn't able to think of anything at all.

Eleven

"**O**kay, people," U of S football coach Herbie Leadman spat into the gym microphone. "In approximately four hours, a guy in a Brooks Brothers suit is gonna come up here and try to tell us we deserve to get the budget ax."

"Booooo!" the entire U of S football team roared.

Melissa glanced down from her perch at the top of the bleachers. It looked like the football players' sagging bench was about to collapse under the weight of their thick thighs and monster-sized torsos. Behind them sat a familiar assortment of star athletes. The basketball players were practically swallowing their knees on the tight bleachers, and the broad-shouldered volleyball players were playfully batting a ball back and forth.

Leadman pulled his belt up and glared at the assembled crowd. "This department *carries* this institution of learning on its back." He balled up his fist and sneered at it. "It's your sweat—and mine—that keeps the U of S on the map. That sells the tickets. That keeps the fat-cat alums coming back with their wallets."

There was a murmur of approval.

"That's why I want to see every one of you at the meeting this afternoon." He pointed at his team. "This isn't just for drill, folks. They're gonna be using live ammo out there. And we're going to be ready for this punk."

"All right!" The crowd let out a roar of solidarity.

"We can beat this."

"Yeeaaahhh."

"We're gonna throw everything we've got at this guy."

"Yeeaaahhh."

Melissa felt the satisfying rumble of three hundred sets of athletic shoes pounding the wooden bleachers. A small thrill tickled her inside. The thunderous, hollow sound of pounding feet and cheering reminded her of high school, and the indoor track practice they used to have in the gym on rainy days.

Melissa looped her short hair behind her ears and stared out at the heads below her. There was something comforting in the familiar pregame, pep-talk feel of the meeting. She liked the snarly sound of the coach's voice and the mounting energy in the room. It was as if everything in the world had been boiled down into two blissfully simple options: win or lose. No maybes. No misunderstandings. No hard-to-read messages or complicated feelings. Just win or lose. Plain and simple.

Melissa stirred in her seat as the track-and-field coach took the mike and began a tirade similar to Coach Leadman's. It was just like old times.

After all, Melissa thought, flexing her fists instinctively, *winning is everything. When you're a winner, it doesn't really matter what your problems are. You're just wanted. Needed. Respected.*

Melissa leaned back on her elbows and surveyed the audience again with appreciation. Then her eye caught a familiar head of curly blond hair. It was Brooks, looking in her direction. He gave her a short wave and stood up. She looked quickly down, her heart dropping into her stomach. Melissa wanted to disappear. But when she looked

up again, Brooks had made his way up the crowd-
ed aisle and was staring down at her. "Hi,
Melissa," Brooks said. "It's, uh, been a while."

"Hi," Melissa managed. It seemed strange to see
Brooks, so distant and formal. The last time she'd
talked to him was just before their wedding—
when she'd felt closer to him than she'd felt to
anyone in her life.

Brooks looked serious. Wearing a pair of jersey
shorts, an unraveling soccer shirt, and a pair of
calf-length socks over his sturdy legs, he looked
just like the all-American nice guy she'd fallen in
love with so many months before. But something
was different.

"May I sit down?" Brooks asked stiffly.

Melissa reached for her workout bag and stuffed
it under her feet. Then she shrugged. "Sure."

She glanced to the front of the meeting. The U
of S's businesslike athletic director was taking the
mike, and the mood had settled down.

Brooks was staring intently at his hands, clasped
together and slung between his muscular legs.
"Melissa, I came to apologize."

Melissa stirred. She didn't know how she felt.
Angry? Relieved? Grateful? There was something
in Brooks's voice that made her uneasy.

"I should have tried to talk with you before

this," Brooks continued. "The letter I wrote you was probably not enough." He coughed and stirred uneasily in his seat.

"No, it wasn't," Melissa answered, looking straight ahead.

Brooks shrugged. "Maybe I don't really know how I feel, Mel. I just knew right then—at the wedding—that I wasn't ready to get married." There was a pause. "To anyone."

"I see," Melissa said in a small voice.

"Melissa?" She felt Brook's solid hand on her shoulder. "I want you to know that I'm really proud of you."

Melissa cringed.

"You've done a lot with your life," Brooks droned on. "You should be proud of your running and your grades. I hope I haven't done anything that would interfere with all that. I just . . . just . . ."

"What?" Melissa turned sharply toward him. She was beginning to wonder why he'd bothered to talk to her at all. His words and tone reminded her of lectures given by her high-school principal. Only this was Brooks. The Brooks she had been ready to pledge her life to, only a few weeks before.

Brooks winced. "It's just that Josh and Winnie are awfully worried about you."

"Oh." Melissa gave him a challenging look. "I think I understand. Josh told you to talk to me, didn't he? He told you I was in a bad way."

Brooks nodded nervously. "Yeah, Melissa, he did. He said you were involved in some thefts around campus. I want you to know that I understand. You were upset with me. It's a natural reaction to do something rash. You wanted attention."

Melissa wanted to cover her ears.

"I do understand," Brooks repeated patronizingly.

Melissa clapped her hands together with finality, faked a smile, and desperately tried to think of a way to change the subject. "Thanks, Brooks. So— what about you? How's life?"

"Well," Brooks said solemnly, though his tone had perked up a bit. "Soccer's keeping me pretty busy. I'm captain of the team now. And I'm doing pretty well in Honor's College, and—"

"Great." Melissa stood up suddenly and reached for her bag. "I've got to run."

"Wait." Brooks's face dropped. Quickly, he dug into his pants pocket and pulled out a little white business card. "Um, Melissa? I hope you don't mind, but I took the liberty of making an appointment for you with a—uh—counselor over at the health center."

Melissa fiddled with the straps on her workout bag. Then she took the card out of Brooks's hand and read it. *Marilyn H. Penrose, Ph.D. Individual and Group Counselor. University of Springfield Health Center.*

"Talk to someone, Melissa," Brooks said. "This Dr. Penrose is supposed to be excellent."

Melissa flinched. She knew she needed help, but there was something in Brooks's superior air that made her want to throw the card in his face.

Instead, Melissa slipped the card in her bag. "You're too kind, Brooks. See you around," she called out over her shoulder as she made her way slowly down the bleachers and out of the meeting. She didn't know what was worse—keeping Brooks's humiliating appointment, or allowing her crazy, out-of-control feelings of despair and confusion to rule her life.

Twelve

A few hours later, Eric Sutter's office was whirring with activity. Rosalyn was hastily making two hundred photocopies of the athletic-budget proposal while Trevor and Phillip were arguing over how to print out a spread sheet from the computer.

Courtney was waiting patiently outside Eric's office door, her heart thumping in her throat.

The athletes' meeting was due to begin soon, and she still hadn't been able to talk to Eric. Trembling in her hand was a smooth white envelope containing the letter of complaint she'd written to him the night before. She wanted him to know how badly he'd behaved. She wanted him to know that she wouldn't allow him to harass her.

Eric's door suddenly flew open and Courtney stepped back.

"Everybody ready for war?" Eric strode into the outer office, smiling and rubbing his hands together, as if he were relishing every minute of the conflict.

There were groans and sighs.

Courtney stepped up. "Eric? May I speak to you for a moment in your office?"

Eric gave her a serious look and glanced at his watch. "Of course. Hope it's about something important."

"Yes, it is," Courtney replied, her face straight and her gaze even.

Courtney followed and closed his office door while Eric settled on the edge of his desk, his arms folded.

"So," he began briskly, his eyes flickering over her lavender jacket and matching skirt. "What can I help you with?"

"I—"

"You missed a great dinner, by the way," he interrupted. "Nice restaurant for such a slowpoke town. Wish you could have been there."

Courtney couldn't believe it. Didn't he get it?

She held the envelope out. "Please read this."

"Okay," he said agreeably, sliding his thumb under the flap and starting to read her complaint with amusement. Then, slowly, his face began to get red. He looked up at her coldly. "Are you kidding?" he sneered.

Courtney looked coolly back at him. "No, I'm not."

"What is this?" He turned the letter and examined the other side. "Some kind of fancy way of saying you don't want to see me?" He glanced at the page again and read. "'Your advances toward me have been unsolicited, inappropriate, and unwanted. They have interfered with our professional working relationship and . . .'" he mocked. "Give me a goddamned break."

"I would like to continue the internship," Courtney said, undeterred. "But I need to be clear about our personal relationship."

Courtney watched in horror as Eric pretended to listen seriously, while slowly ripping her complaint in two.

"You really are a piece of work," he concluded, chuckling while he released the torn halves.

Courtney shuddered as they floated slowly into the wastepaper basket below.

"I'm a busy man, Courtney." Eric glared at her.

"You know that better than anyone. So if you think I have time for a college girl's nonsense, I've misjudged you."

"What do you mean by that?" Courtney shot back. She reached for the file cabinet to steady her hand.

"What I mean is—you're going to have to grow up," he snapped, glancing at his watch. "Here we are, a few short minutes away from a very important meeting, and you're sidetracking me with your personal life."

"*My* personal life . . . ?" Courtney began.

"Listen." Eric stood up, pointing at her. "Don't play this game. I hired you and you owe me a little loyalty."

"Loyalty?"

"I'm warning you. If I find out that you've been spreading hysterical stories . . ." He cut his sentence short, shaking his head angrily.

Courtney crossed her arms. "Are you threatening me?"

He held his hand up, as if to silence her. Then he lowered his voice into a growl. "If you say anything about this ridiculous accusation to *anyone*, I will happily flunk you. Then, I will make it my business to make sure your transcript contains a rather bad letter of review."

Courtney was so taken aback, she began stumbling for words. "How could . . . You can't . . ." she stammered.

"Oh, no? Try me." Eric relaxed his face. Courtney stared at him with fury as he began stepping toward her. He was like an actor who'd turned the pages of his script and was suddenly working on a new scene. It took her breath away. "I know all this stuff is a turn-on for you. Why don't you let yourself go?"

"All I want is to get through this internship without problems."

"Okay." Eric held his hands up. "I have a proposal. Maybe we can both come away from this situation happy."

Courtney had stepped away from him as far as she could. Her back was now up against the door to the office, and someone had started knocking.

"Let's go, Eric," Trevor said. "Fifteen minutes until the meeting."

"Be right there," Eric called out gaily before he focused again on Courtney. "After the meeting you're coming back to my place with me."

Courtney felt her knees buckling.

"We'll have a little fun." He stepped closer and snaked a finger through her hair. "Up close and personal. Then, you're off the hook. Back to business. And you get what might possibly be the best recommendation ever written—to any grad school in the country."

Before Courtney could say a word, he'd reached out, opened the door, and walked out.

Sick at heart, Courtney followed him, grabbed her notes, and began following the group across campus to the university gymnasium.

By the time Courtney, Eric, and the rest of the interns had taken their seats behind a long table in front of the bleachers, the gym was jammed with noisy athletes, school officials, and local business-men wearing dark suits and U of S booster hats. All of the seats were taken, and the university's maintenance crew was rolling out another set of bleachers.

Holding her head high, Courtney prayed that she would be able to get through the meeting. "Good afternoon, everyone," she said, holding the mike in her hand. Her gaze traveled over the hun-dreds of angry faces and finally froze on the front row, where Dash and Lauren sat together, along with the rest of the reporters.

"Boooooo!" the crowd immediately came back.

Courtney narrowed her eyebrows in shock. She looked over at Eric, who shrugged.

"No pay, no play. No pay, no play," the football

section began to chant. "No pay, no play. No pay, no play. No pay, no play."

Courtney looked around the room. Even the coaches were joining in. A few of the local businessmen were clapping and jauntily keeping time to the chant with their elbows.

Courtney tried to smile and act as if she were used to handling crowds like this. She held up her hand and waved it good-naturedly. "Good afternoon!" she repeated, hearing the noise die down a little. "I'm Courtney Conner . . ."

"We know!" someone yelled back.

"I'm the regents' student liaison in this budget matter, and I'm here to introduce Mr. Eric Sutter, who will be happy to explain the proposal to you and answer your questions."

"Booooooo!" the crowd roared back. Courtney sat down, sick at heart.

Eric took the mike and was about to speak when Coach Leadman stood up in the bleachers. "We're a goddamned money machine for this institution, and we're not going to take this lousy treatment from outsiders like you!"

"Yeeaahhhhh!" the crowd roared.

Courtney looked over. Unlike Wednesday's meeting, Eric wasn't his usual cool self. She watched him rub the back of his neck and stand there helplessly in front of the crowd.

"Uh, yes, Coach Leadman," Eric began haltingly, as if he were unable to focus. "In fact, we did go over those figures on net revenues from football events . . ."

"Yeah, I hope you did, because, listen, buster . . . " Leadman began arguing.

"Courtney?" Eric turned to her, handing her the mike. Courtney's heart stopped. "Would you take over for a minute while I dig up those figures?"

"I—uh," Courtney stammered, watching helplessly as Eric returned to his seat and began flipping aimlessly through a stack of papers.

"Boooooooo!"

"I have a few questions for you, Courtney," she heard a sharp voice yelling from the front. She glanced across the table and saw that it was Lauren, holding a reporter's notepad. Dressed in a pair of form-fitting jeans and a black T-shirt that read U of S Women's Political Caucus, Lauren looked more like a hardened activist than the mousy Tri Beta hopeful she'd been last fall.

Courtney gave her a weak smile. "Yes?"

"What really burns the women athletes," Lauren began in an insulting tone, "is that their team budgets have *always* been pitiful compared to the big bucks spent on men's sports."

"Booooooo!" the football boosters roared back.

"May I speak?" Lauren shrieked at the top of her lungs, instantly silencing them. "I've spent some time covering the subject for the *Journal* and I happen to know that this budget," Lauren slapped the proposal she was holding in her hand, "is going to keep a lot of women from state competition. It will kill their travel budgets. But it will be like a flea bite to men's football and basketball."

"That's true," Courtney began in earnest, "but the proposal seeks to be fair by—"

"This budget is an affront to every single woman athlete at this university," Lauren screamed.

Courtney's eyes looked desperately in Eric's direction, but he remained behind the table, still flipping through papers and pondering numbers.

"How can you—as a woman—back these guys up, Courtney?" Lauren challenged her.

"Yeah!" the entire U of S women's basketball team cheered. The gymnasium was beginning to thunder as the crowd began stomping on the bleachers. Courtney started to shake with anger. What right did they have to treat her this way? They acted as if she were personally responsible for the university's financial problems.

"I guess you don't really care, though," Lauren persisted. "It's not like the Tri Betas have any women who are interested in anything except tennis and croquet."

Courtney's mouth went dry. Eric's attack on her character had been enough for her to handle in one afternoon. Now Lauren was abusing her.

"I'd like to know how much the regents are paying you to stand up there," Courtney heard a familiar voice call out. Her eyes dropped down to the front row, near Lauren. It was Dash.

"Did they think we'd put up with this unfairness in women's sports just because they've put a woman up there to defend it?" Dash jeered her.

Dash too? Why was she suddenly everyone's favorite enemy?

"Can we get back to the subject at hand?" Courtney said firmly, though her hands were beginning to tremble and she could feel the perspiration starting to trickle down her neck. "Mr. Sutter is ready now to help you . . ."

"Don't you think it's time to even things up between men and women?" Dash continued to badger her.

"I—I . . ." Courtney began to stammer. Looking over at Eric, she could see that he had no intention of leaping to her defense. He was perfectly happy to hang her out to dry before a crowd of several hundred angry students.

"Do you think it's *fair*?" Dash asked again.

Courtney looked across at Dash's black eyes and angry face. She could also see Lauren looking at him with surprise and pride. Suddenly, the large room became very small and quiet and still. Her swirling, confused thoughts became focused. Everything around her blurred. Everything inside of her hardened into a single moment of clarity.

Fair? Fair? Fair? The end of Dash's question echoed in her mind. They were asking her about fairness when every single person in the room was trying to use her for their own purposes?

"Things between men and women are rarely fair," Courtney heard her voice return sharply. Inside, she felt as if she had fallen through space until she had finally hit something. Now, everything—her frustration, her anger, her guilt—was spilling out uncontrollably.

Courtney's head was nodding angrily as the crowd began to quiet. "Right. You all look at me as if I don't know a thing about unfairness. But I have first-hand experience."

The crowd looked stunned.

"Take my work here." Courtney jerked her head in Eric's direction. "This man. The famous financial expert, Eric Sutter, who's supposed to be addressing you this afternoon, he thinks that because he's a man, he can control me. Overpower me. Bully me."

Courtney saw Eric get up. "You're burying yourself if you continue," he whispered in her ear. "Shut up!"

But something inside Courtney was urging her on. At that moment, nothing was more important to her than the truth—no matter what the consequences were.

"Why do you all look so surprised?" Courtney shouted over the crowd. "The women's basketball team has it rough. Okay. But if you really want to talk unfair, take a look at how my boss is treating me. I have an internship for credit with this guy. He's using it to grope me and take advantage of the situation."

"Stop it Courtney," Eric hissed. "You're going too far."

"Just minutes ago," Courtney continued to shout, "he threatened to sabotage my career unless I agreed to sleep with him. It's called sexual harassment, everyone. And it's not a game that ends when the whistle blows. It's a game that goes on all day, every day. For millions of women. Welcome to the real world. Welcome to *my* world."

There was a gasp from the crowd. Courtney turned to Eric, who looked as white as a sheet.

Suddenly, the reporters in the front row were scribbling madly to get her quotes. Flashbulbs were popping.

And Courtney knew that no matter what happened, her life would never be the same again.

Thirteen

L iza had numbers on the brain.

"Okay." She fanned her raspberry-polished nails down a column of figures. "Round-trip ticket to L.A.: four hundred thirty-six dollars. Six nights at the fabulous Palm Court Motel: two hundred eighty-five dollars."

"Don't forget transportation," Faith reminded her, taking a bite of her oatmeal. She looked across the dining-commons table at Kimberly, who was groggily stirring sugar into her coffee cup. "Right?"

Kimberly rested her cheek tiredly on her hand.

"The last time I was in L.A., I spent so much money it took years for my savings account to recover."

Liza dropped her rhinestone-studded wing-tipped sunglasses and bit her lip nervously. "Really?"

"New York's expensive too, but at least there's the subway," Faith explained, her eye catching something on the front page of the new Tuesday *Weekly*. "In L.A., you've got to rent a car or spend a fortune on taxis."

Liza nervously twisted the dangling black cords on her eyeglasses and scribbled something in her notepad. "Right. I'll budget a hundred bucks for that." Then she smiled ecstatically into space. "Of course, Rich's dad will probably send a limo to meet me at the airport. You know how these things work."

Faith looked up at Liza with concern. "This is going to be an expensive trip. Are you sure you can afford it?"

Liza tallied up her numbers again and sighed. "If I don't eat a thing, it will cost me about nine hundred bucks." She checked her bankbook balance again. "And I've got exactly nine hundred four-teen dollars and fifty-six cents to my name. So it's fate."

"I just hope it's the fate you'd planned on."
Kimberly shook her head and gulped her coffee.

Liza leaned back and stretched her arms up to
the ceiling, wiggling her bright nails in the air.
"It's my own personal fairy tale come true, actually. You should see the arrangements Rich and
Mr. Greenberg are making for me." Liza picked
up the letter Mr. Greenberg had sent her
through Rich and looked at it for the thou-
sandth time.

"If you read that one more time," Faith said,
laughing, "it's going to burn itself permanently
into your retinas."

But Liza couldn't help herself. She sighed and
stared at the expensive stationery. "Bernard
Greenberg Productions, Incorporated. 1-0–0–9–8
Taylor Street, Hollywood, California. Screen test,
ten o'clock. Meeting with top Hollywood agent
Maury Belden, one o'clock . . ."

"I'm really happy for you, Liza," Faith said, patting her on the back.

Liza continued to beam. For a while, she had
almost tried not to believe it was really happening
to her. If it hadn't been true, it would have been
too painfully disappointing. "The best part about
this whole thing," Liza said, dreamily biting into a
large cinnamon bun, "is that Rich is doing it for

me. He must love me very much to go to all this trouble."

Faith gave Liza an encouraging smile.

"So, Faith," Kimberly piped up. "You're going to be alone in your room for a week."

"Uh-huh." Faith nodded, narrowing her eyebrows with interest over the *Weekly.*

"Perfect." Kimberly stabbed the air with her coffee spoon. "Next week is the Coed-by-Bed experiment in Coleridge. Just think, you could sign up for a mystery male roommate."

"No way."

Kimberly giggled. "I'll sign you up myself."

"Check this out," Faith murmured. "Did you see this sexual harassment story in the *Weekly* about Courtney and Eric Sutter?"

"Oooo," Liza squeaked. "Scandal. It makes my heart go pitter-patter. Lemmie see."

Faith shook her head as she calmly pulled the paper out of Liza's reach. "KC told me that Courtney was having trouble with him—and that she broke down last week when she was addressing the athletes over the budget. But now here's Eric Sutter's denial printed up."

Kimberly shook her head too. "Things are just so complicated between men and women. I think we should have separate universities. Separate office buildings. Separate countries, even. Then we'd all get along just fine."

"Hmm," Liza thought out loud. "The end of the human race. Party's over, folks. No more fun and games. What a boring way to end it all."

"I can't believe Courtney would make something like that up," Faith muttered, playing with her braid thoughtfully as she closed the paper.

"Mmm," Liza spun the front page around excitedly to see the story. "Who knows? Maybe she thought she could just hook her claws into him and get a ride to the top. When he shrugs her off, she gets even."

Faith looked at Liza sternly. "That's absolutely ridiculous. Courtney doesn't need anyone's help to the top. She's smart, determined, and sensible. Everyone knows that."

Liza shrugged cheerfully, pushing the paper over to Kimberly. "Well, it was a great theory while it lasted."

"In fact, Courtney was the one who figured out how to get KC away from those druggies she was hanging out with," Faith insisted. "She's a good person, and I can't believe she'd pull a trick like this."

Kimberly's head was shaking gently as she scanned the page. "This Eric Sutter doesn't fool around. He absolutely denies harassing Courtney. Listen to his statement:

" 'I find it outrageous that the news media has publicized these allegations, despite the fact that Miss Conner hasn't a shred of evidence to back her story. Common criminals are treated better than this. Miss Conner's charges are, sadly, the result of injured feelings on her part. During her internship with me, she apparently developed a romantic attachment to me, which I naturally discouraged. Psychiatric experts could tell us more, I'm sure. But she's a troubled young woman seeking revenge.' "

"Right," Faith said with a disgusted look.

"He's going to get a hearing before the Dean of Students," Kimberly read on. "Listen to this.

" 'I have requested an immediate hearing. It is imperative that I clear myself of this outrageous charge and get on with the more important business of the university's financial situation. Neither my reputation nor the university's deserves to be tarnished by the delusions of this sad young woman.' "

"Eeew." Liza held her nose. "I hate him already. Guys who talk like that give me the creeps."

"Guys like that run the world, Liza," Faith said quietly.

"It all comes down to who you want to believe," Kimberly added softly.

"Would you guys tone it down?" Greg Sukamaki was calling out, waving his arms for order in the *Weekly* newsroom that same morning.

"She's a sorority nutcase," one of the sports writers was gloating. "Wigged out over a lousy date."

"Put a lid on it, Arnett," a senior writer from the women's political caucus barked back. "It's obvious Courtney Conner was bullied by that idiot and she's not going to take it ."

"Okay, everyone," Greg continued, his hands planted on his hips as if he were about to send warriors into battle. "You did a crackerjack job on the Sutter harassment story for this week's edition. But I've called this emergency meeting because I want to make some special assignments. Remember, the Sutter-Conner hearing is the day after tomorrow."

There was a murmur of excitement among the staff, who were lounging on stacks of papers, desks, and overturned recycle cans.

Dash slid his eyes over to Lauren, who was glaring defiantly into space. Her hair was frizzed out today and her newly slender body was draped confidently across the top of an overstuffed chair at the front of the room.

"This is probably the year's top story, guys," Greg continued, pacing back and forth. "Sutter must be a real hotshot, because the wires are using it and it will probably rate a spot on regional television news at the very least. So I want a first-class effort. Richard and Alison, I want you to stay with the lead story. Lauren, I want a sidebar on national trends, statistics—anything you can find on harassment that would work for this."

There was a pause as Greg's eyes hung on Dash's face momentarily, then dropped.

Dash flinched. He knew what Greg was thinking. Greg wasn't going to assign him to the story because he'd been personally involved with Courtney. It would be a conflict of interest.

"Come on, Greg," Richard suddenly called out, jerking his head back in Dash's direction. "We all know that Dash knows Courtney. Why beat around the bush?" He turned around and gave Dash a pleading look. "Dash? We need background on this. How about helping us out?"

Dash stirred uneasily on his perch—a low file cabinet near the copy machine in the center of the newsroom. The noisy room went silent and all eyes were suddenly glued to him.

"Come on, buddy," Richard was urging him. "No one can reach her for an interview. She's hiding out somewhere. So we don't have a handle on her side of the story. You dated her, so what gives?"

Dash glanced over at Lauren, who quickly turned her head away. Then he shrugged. "Yeah, but what of it?"

"Well, what did you think of Sutter's statement?" Richard wanted to know. "Is she the kind of person who'd get delusional? I mean, is she wacko or what?"

The room was silent.

Dash swallowed. The Courtney he knew was a total ditzoid. She'd been obsessive, hysterical, and unbalanced to the max. Plus, he knew for a fact that she'd had some kind of involvement with Sutter. He had seen it with his own eyes in Sutter's office.

Still, Dash thought, Courtney deserved the benefit of the doubt. She was a person he had once admired—had once been attracted to. For all he knew, she could be telling the truth. He had no right to incriminate her.

Finally, Dash looked up and shrugged. He took a gulp of his coffee. "I don't know, Richard. I just don't know."

There was a collective groan in the room, and Greg made a move to close the meeting. Across the room, Dash could see that Lauren was headed his way. She was shaking her head in disgust.

"Why are you protecting her?" Lauren asked, her hand on her hip.

Dash leaned back, trying not to stare too deeply into her violet eyes. He felt his lips part involuntarily. Lauren looked more beautiful than he'd ever seen her.

"I'm *not* protecting anyone, Lauren," Dash replied, trying to sound confident and casual. He gingerly reached out to touch her belt.

"It doesn't seem that way to me," Lauren shot back, snapping her book bag over her shoulder. She glanced down at his hand as if it were an annoying insect. "I thought you were over her."

"I *am*," Dash insisted. "I am." He hiked his shoulders self-consciously. He was no longer Teflon Guy. He was just a guy in love. A guy who would do practically anything to make this girl fall in love with him again.

"Listen, Lauren," Dash said, glancing around the room to make sure no one was listening. "Courtney and I did not have a relationship . . ."

"Right. I suppose I imagined the two of you kissing? That I never saw her at your apartment?"

Dash bit back the urge to argue with her. He stared at the smooth white skin on her arm and remembered its slippery smooth feel in the pool.

"Not a relationship the way we would define it."

Lauren gave him a challenging look that was somewhere between a tease and a question. "How would we define it, Dash?"

Dash coughed. "Um. Well. We were close. I thought. We talked. We did things together that we cared about. You know . . ."

"Yes."

"Courtney . . ." he began awkwardly, but with determination. "You've got to understand this, Lauren. Courtney just flat out went after me. I don't know why. She had some crazy attraction to me. And I fell into it. For a while, anyway."

"Oh," Lauren said, a little embarrassed.

"It didn't take me long to figure out that we didn't have much in common," Dash continued. "I tried to cool things off, but she wouldn't take no for an answer. She kept following me. Calling me at all hours. And then, when I really called it quits, she flipped out."

Lauren's mouth fell open. "So. There's our proof."

"There's more."

"What?"

"Last week, I saw her in Sutter's office," Dash said. He almost felt guilty for telling Lauren. "They were definitely together."

"She's crazy."

"Lauren."

"She manipulates men, then lies about it," Lauren shot back. "Just because she has a closet full of conservative suits and a string of pearls doesn't mean she's straight. She's a nutcase."

Dash flopped his forehead into his hand. Lauren was tough, but he knew he had to stand firm. "Maybe she did act like a nutcase with me. But that doesn't prove she lied about Sutter."

Lauren rolled her eyes. "Well, not exactly, I suppose, but I think you should testify at the hearing."

"Against her?"

"The Dean of Students is inviting character witnesses to submit written testimony. Just tell the truth about her. It's a character question."

Dash instinctively reached his hand out for Lauren's. "But I don't know what the truth is. Don't you see?"

Lauren hardened her eyes, stood up, and slipped her hand out of his grip. Then she reached for her book-bag strap and turned toward the door. "Yes,

I think I do see, Dash. I think you're still involved with her, in a way. You're trying to protect her. I'm sorry. I'll just never understand."

For an instant, Dash wanted to throw himself down at Lauren's feet and beg her to understand. Instead, he watched, cemented to his seat on the file cabinet, as Lauren stepped briskly out of the newsroom.

He felt the blood drain out of his face. His miserable life without Lauren flashed before his eyes. Did he care what was right anymore? Or what was true? Did it matter if he didn't have Lauren? She was the only thing he cared about now. So before he could think, he was leaping across the newsroom and up the staircase. He reached Lauren just as she was opening the door.

"Okay," Dash panted.

"Okay what?" Lauren stared back at him curiously.

"I'll do it," he breathed. "I'll file written testimony. I'll go to the hearing. And . . ." he gave Lauren a frightened look. "And then we'll go from there."

Lauren shrugged and echoed his words. "And then we'll go from there."

Fourteen

···

*L*ater that night, Josh was slumped in the bluish light of his home computer screen, holding his soda can over his mouth. He shook out the last few drops.

Tap. Tap. Tap.

He erased the last of Rich's documents from the screen. Then he made a backup copy of the homework assignment he'd just finished for his upper-division programming class.

Josh stared out the funky dormer window above his desk and sighed. Down the hall, he could hear the faint sounds of a new jazz CD Clifford had just bought. Rich was studying in the kitchen and

Winnie had just left for the bathroom.

Beep. The computer reminded him to save his last document. Josh sullenly punched a series of buttons and slipped in a game disk. Then he sat back and stared up at the dark sky through the window.

Josh was worried.

For the last week, Winnie had been sick every day. First it was just dizziness. But then it turned into a total weariness. Then nausea. At this point, Winnie was doing little more than lying in bed all day, trying not to move.

Josh played uneasily with his keyboard, then impatiently flicked off the power.

Whatever Winnie had, it had completely changed her, Josh concluded. He let out a sigh. These days Winnie could barely move out of bed. Her hair was a pathetic-looking nest of spikes, and she'd given up wearing anything but beat-up T-shirts, baggy sweatpants, and a worn-out pair of fuzzy slippers.

So far, he hadn't been able to get her to the health center. And though he'd tried to diagnose her illness with a medical reference book, he couldn't find anything that matched her symptoms.

Suddenly there was a loud thump from the bath-room.

Josh yelled, lunging for the bathroom door. He found Winnie draped over the edge of the bathtub, her cheek pressed to its smooth surface. He gasped when he saw her face. It was deathly white. Her eyes were two dark circles.

"Oh . . . I'm just . . ." Winnie began mumbling.

There was a lump in Josh's throat. "Winnie? What happened?"

"I think I fell over," Winnie whispered, moving her legs sluggishly on the yellow tile floor as if she were thinking of getting up, but couldn't. "I—felt—dizzy and a little—uh—sick."

"Here," Josh slipped his arm around her. "I'm going to get you back to bed." Winnie's T-shirt slid up her leg as he got ready to move her, revealing a dark purple bruise on the side of her thigh. Josh drew back and paled.

"Wha—what's wrong?" Winnie asked wearily, slowly raising her head and sliding her knees up.

"Win . . ." Josh said numbly. "That bruise . . ."

Winnie looked down limply. "Oooh. Right you are."

His heart thumping with worry, Josh lowered himself down so that he was sitting next to Winnie on the cool tile floor. He was staring at the top of the toilet seat, but his mind was on the medical textbook he'd been reading.

Winnie groaned. "Just let me sit here—for a minute. If I—move I know I'll . . ."

"It's okay. It's okay," Josh whispered back. He had to think.

Leukemia. An almost uniformly fatal cancerous disease characterized by excessive production of white blood cells, and often accompanied by severe anemia.

Josh looked over at Winnie's chalky gray face.

Symptoms may include excessive fatigue, nausea, and bruising of the skin.

"No," Josh said softly.

"Huh?" Winnie made an effort to turn her head. "Josh? Would you stay with me?"

"Yeah." Josh felt his voice squeak. He coughed. His eyes were beginning to tear up—a little like the day he had gotten married. Quickly, he brushed his cheek against his arm. Then he cleared his throat again. "Yes. I'll always stay with you."

There was a long silence as Josh sat next to Winnie, listening to the steady drip of the tub faucet, not daring to tell her what he'd been thinking.

He felt Winnie's head drop down on his shoulder. "Okay," she whispered.

"Win?"

"Yeah?"

"I'm going to make you go to the doctor now."

Winnie sighed. "I knew you were going to say that."

Josh felt his chest heaving. His throat was tightening up, and tears were beginning to slide down his face. He knew he couldn't hold it in. He dropped his head down in his arms and sobbed.

"Josh?" Winnie's voice got a little stronger. "Josh. What's wrong?"

He lifted his head and looked at her through his wet tears. "You've got to go to the doctor, Win. There could be something seriously wrong with you."

A frightened look swept over Winnie's small, peaked face. "What do you mean?"

"Just do it."

"What makes you think it's something serious?" Winnie asked.

Josh's face was twisted up so badly he could barely talk. "The bruising, nausea, tiredness . . . you could have some kind of blood disease. I just want you to check it out."

Winnie looked stunned.

"It could be something like mononucleosis, or hepatitis, or—or even leukemia . . ." Josh said. "We have to find out."

"Okay." There was a catch in Winnie's soft voice. "I'll go see the doctor."

Josh drew her close and held her tight. The

doctor's diagnosis couldn't come soon enough. Every second was going to be agony until he knew for sure that Winnie was going to be healthy again.

"I can't figure it out." KC was pacing back and forth across her tiny dorm room in Langston Hall.

Courtney looked hopelessly up at her and Cody, then slumped back down on the bed. Her blond hair was pulled back into a clumpy ponytail, and her polo shirt had a mayonnaise stain on it from the sandwich KC had brought her earlier. All day long, she'd been in hiding from her sorority sisters. She knew they'd been gossiping about her nonstop since the athletes' meeting.

"The harassment hearing isn't until tomorrow," KC muttered, handing Courtney a tissue, which she waved away. "How could the entire campus already know the awful things Dash is going to say about you?"

Courtney shook her head.

Cody snapped open a can of juice and handed it to Courtney. Then he turned and looked out the window. "Dash spends a lot of time with other reporters. Someone must have gotten hold of a copy of his written testimony and spread it around."

"But where is Dash coming up with this stuff?" KC demanded. "And why?"

"I don't know." Courtney's voice was shaking with anger. "I know I came on too strong to Dash and he didn't like it. I was pretty carried away, KC. But it doesn't have anything to do with Eric Sutter. Nothing at all!"

KC flicked her hair back impatiently. "But why is Dash being so vindictive? Everyone says he's turning you into something from *Fatal Attraction*—as if you were some kind of emotional basket case who seduces men, then turns on them."

Courtney gave a bitter smile. "Funny to think that I was attracted to Dash because of his honesty. He didn't seem to have a dishonest bone in his body."

Cody shrugged and turned back to face Courtney. "He doesn't, Courtney. He's a straight-arrow."

"Cody!" KC protested, shocked. "How can you defend him?"

Cody shoved his hands in his pockets, leaned against the window ledge, and crossed his cowboy boots. "Because I know him. And I know he's a good guy."

Courtney narrowed her eyes. "He's making a mistake."

"Maybe he's trying to tell the truth," Cody said gently.

KC was staring angrily at Cody as Courtney slammed down her can of juice. "Look, Dash is taking one moment out of my life. One crazy moment. And he's using it to try to show everyone I'm capable of incredible dishonesty."

"Why would Courtney make up a story like that?" KC reproached Cody. "What could she possibly gain by charging a prominent guy like Eric Sutter with sexual harassment?"

Cody looked down at the toe of his boot thoughtfully. Then he got up and walked across the room, sitting down near Courtney. "I'm not saying Dash is right or wrong. I'm just sayin' that Dash is an honest guy. You've got to understand, Courtney. Things don't look good for the hearing tomorrow. It's just your word against Sutter's. And he doesn't just have Dash testifying against your character. He's got an army of people who'll defend him to the last, just to protect their own backsides."

"I am not lying," Courtney broke out, her voice rising with conviction.

Cody's eyes were pleading. "I think you should consider dropping the charges. Go easy on yourself, Courtney. Get on with the rest of your life while you still can."

"Cody!" KC blasted him.

"I haven't done anything wrong and I refuse to act as if I did," Courtney declared, standing up and crossing her arms angrily. "No one can get me to back down now. I want this thing out in the open. I want to tell the truth about what can happen to women when they work with slime like Eric Sutter."

"I completely agree," KC said instantly, moving toward Courtney and glaring at Cody.

"The odds are not good that anyone will believe me," Courtney said, staring bravely ahead. "But I'll just have to take the consequences, whatever they are."

KC put her arm around Courtney's shoulder. "Is there anything I can do?"

Courtney sighed and reached for her purse. "Thanks. But I think I'm going to go over to the Forsythe Building and clean out my desk. Maybe Eric will be there. Maybe if I confront him one last time . . ."

"He'll listen to reason," KC finished her sentence, leading her to the door. There was a determined smile of solidarity on her face.

Courtney banged her fist against the doorjamb. "I just can't believe a man of his education and stature would tell such lies. It's still hard for me to believe."

"You can spend the night here, Courtney," KC offered, "if you want to stay clear of the Tri Betas."

Courtney smiled. "Thanks. I'll think about it."

Right after KC shut the door to the hall, she spun around and faced Cody. He was just behind her, reaching a long arm around her waist and bending his head down to kiss her.

KC pushed him away. "How could you!"

Cody bent his head a little to the side, his caramel eyes glued to hers. For a moment, his lips had the trace of a smile. Then his expression turned serious. "I'm sorry, KC. I call them as I see them."

KC stood staring at Cody's face, her hand planted on her hip like a pistol she was ready to shoot. "How could you even *think* of suggesting that she drop the charges?"

"It might be the best thing," he said simply.

"Oh, it might?" KC yelled, leaning forward with both hands planted on her back jeans pockets. "Let me tell you something. Courtney is my friend. She's backed me up on more things than I care to tell you. And she is telling the truth."

"Let me get this straight." Cody's eyes traveled up to the ceiling. "She's your friend, and therefore she is telling the truth."

"Right. I know her. And I know that she would tell the truth."

Cody sat down and folded his hands together. "KC. I've told you about the Rosebud Dance."

"Yeah." KC twisted her hands together guiltily. KC had invited Cody to the formal event, but had stood him up after a bad encounter with her mother. "You said she acted weird."

"She acted more than weird." Cody nodded, drawing himself up. "She acted like someone with serious emotional problems. She was screaming and raving, KC. She barely knew what was going on around her. I've seen girls like that. They want to have control over a guy, and if they can't, they go ballistic."

KC exploded. "You're turning this into a witch hunt."

"She had something going on with Sutter," Cody came back. "Dash saw her practically kissing him in his office. And I've heard Sutter talk about her on the telephone in the Peabody Mansion."

"You're a snake," KC yelled at him. "Of course he's bragging about her over the phone, you eavesdropper. He's delusional. He must have thought she actually liked him—the slime bag."

"How can you be sure?" Cody stepped away from her.

"I thought you were loyal," KC accused him.

"I am. I care about you, KC," Cody insisted. "But I won't lie because you want me to protect your friend. If anyone asks me to testify, I'll tell what I know."

"That's big of you."

"I'm interested in the truth."

"Okay," KC came back instantly. "If you're so into the truth, here's a dose of it, specially delivered to you."

Cody closed his eyes. "Let me guess. You don't really like me after all."

KC's face dropped. Then she steadied herself, egged on by her building anger and her frustration. "That's right, Cody," she said lightly. "I was upset last Friday night when I went over to your place. You see, Peter and I didn't just calmly agree to see other people. What happened was that I found out he was cheating on me."

"I see," Cody said, quietly listening.

She pretended to toss her head nonchalantly. "I was just frustrated and mad. Guess I wanted to get back at Peter. So I threw myself at you."

"Oh."

Seething, KC glared at him. "So you see Cody, I don't want to be involved with you at all," KC lied. "You'd be the last person on earth I'd fall for."

Fifteen

"Brrrrr." Dash shook his head and swallowed. "Wainwright, you damn fool, you. You eat peppers like that every night and your stomach will turn into something out of *Night of the Living Dead*."

"Clears the sinuses," Cody replied, flourishing another pepper, dropping it delicately in his mouth, and chewing it.

"Damn." Dash felt the burn in his mouth.

"Watah?" Cody poised a pitcher of ice water over Dash's glass.

"A full glass, please," Dash replied, watching the ice plop into his glass. He scanned the stacks of novels crammed into Cody's many bookcases.

"I'm just trying to pay you back for being my guest in this humble abode. But I guess it's not a good night. In fact, it's a real *stinkuh*, as my folks in Tennessee would say."

"That bad?" Dash asked, getting up to pull out a volume of early Hemingway news articles.

Cody held up his glass as if he were making an important announcement. "Ms. KC Angeletti has given me the . . ." He pretended to cut his throat with his finger.

"Oooh," Dash started. "Bad news. And what was your reply?"

Cody lifted his eyebrows and stared into the distance. "I said, Frankly my dear, I don't give a damn."

Dash laughed as he sat down with the book. "Right."

"She says I'm disloyal to think that charming Courtney Conner is a little bit crazy."

Dash nervously bobbed his ankle up and down on the floor. He knew he'd never get a better chance to ask Cody about testifying at the hearing with him. "Back me up tomorrow, then, will you? You saw her at the Rosebud Dance. She's an emotional three-ring circus."

Cody bit his lip. "You serious?"

"Absolutely," Dash replied, trying to hide the urgency in his voice. "You saw what she was like. I need someone to verify what I'm saying. Otherwise . . ."

Cody frowned at him. "What?"

Dash stirred uncomfortably. *Otherwise what?* He tried to think. *Otherwise I'll look even more like a fool than I already do? Otherwise it will look like I'm just doing it because Lauren wanted me to?*

"You sure about this?" Cody said. "I mean, Courtney might be unstable. But something tells me you've got something more to prove."

Dash felt a pang of guilt.

"Come on, Dash."

Dash grabbed a pepper and stuffed it in his mouth. Then he stood up and began pacing. "Maybe I do."

"Don't tell me," Cody said quietly, following Dash back and forth with his eyes. "It has something to do with big violet eyes. A beautiful face. Someone who wants to be sure about you."

"Lauren's not just another beautiful face," Dash snapped back.

"Whoa." Cody smiled.

"But yeah," Dash admitted. "Lauren is stuck on this idea that Courtney has some kind of hold on me. Testifying against Courtney *was* Lauren's idea.

And now I'm not so sure what I'm after. The truth . . ."

"Or Lauren," Cody finished his sentence with a sigh.

Dash stood up, frustrated, jamming his hands into his jeans pockets. "It's time for me to take off. Show up tomorrow if you want to. I don't even know if I care anymore."

"Okay." Cody stood up and walked out the door with him into the warm spring night.

Outside, crickets were chirping in the soft darkness, and the lights from the Peabody Mansion sent squares of yellow out onto the manicured lawns that surrounded it. Dash and Cody started toward the path between Cody's place and the mansion, which led to the street. They stopped when they heard a door close inside, and voices in the living room.

"Sutter," Cody said, jerking his head in the direction of the window.

Dash hunkered down and moved through the short grass toward the open window, which was high enough for both of them to stand under without being seen. "He's got someone in there with him. A woman."

They ducked closer until their backs were up against the rough brick wall of the mansion.

Inside, they could hear a soft, pleading voice. A smart, direct voice. Dash recognized it with a start.

"It's Courtney," Dash hissed, furrowing his brow in the darkness and straining to hear.

"Hello, Courtney."

"Listen, Eric," Courtney began, "I know my public statement has you backed up against a wall. But—but can't we solve this some other way besides totally destroying my reputation?"

For a moment, Dash was almost relieved. It sounded like she was trying to get him to back off from the hearings to protect her reputation. She was guilty!

Suddenly, Eric must have moved closer to the window, because they could both hear him clearly.

"Ah-ha," Eric replied. "So you've come crawling back."

Courtney pleaded with him. "This thing might blow up in your face. Can't you just shrug it off for now? Tell everyone you'd misunderstood me. Tell them it was all a terrible mistake."

"You think I'm going to tell the board of regents that I have a thing for one of their students?" he sneered. "I may be crazy for you, but I'm not stupid."

Dash and Cody looked at each another.

Eric's cold voice carried clearly in the night air. "Look. You've made the right decision. You've come to pay your bill. Let's go upstairs now before you change your mind."

A chill ran down Dash's back. They heard movement, as if the two were struggling. Then a loud scream.

"No!" Courtney's scream gathered power. "Get away! Can't you see I'm not interested and never have been?"

Dash and Cody ran to the front of the house. All Dash could think was that Courtney was in some kind of danger—maybe even in physical danger. The blood was pounding in his head as he raced down the path behind Cody. But just as they got there, they saw Courtney fling open the front door with one hand, holding her ripped blouse with the other. Then she fled down the dark street, and in an instant she was gone.

Dash looked over at Cody with wide-opened eyes. "She's not lying. The guy's an animal."

Cody nodded. "The truth is out—at last."

Melissa looked carefully over her shoulder as she walked up the front path of the sprawling U of S Health Center. Then she looked down at the small business card in her hand.

Marilyn H. Penrose, Ph.D., Individual and Group Counselor.

She flipped the card over and stared again at Brooks's solid, blocklike lettering. *Thursday, 2 P.M.*

A hollow feeling of dread and humiliation sunk through her. What was she supposed to say to this total stranger? Marilyn H. Penrose. She tried to imagine the woman. Did she wear sensible shoes and a severe bun to match her Ph.D.? Or did she have wild, dark hair and red lips like the beautiful Ph.D. authors on the jackets of the self-esteem books in the student bookstore?

"Just get me through this," Melissa muttered to herself. "Maybe Brooks was right. Maybe I need help. But please let me get through this without seeing anyone I know."

When she reached the glass door entrance, Melissa held her sunglasses on her nose and lowered her head. If she could just make it to the reception desk. Then they'd probably give her a private place to wait, with the other crazy people.

"May I help you?" a cheerful-looking girl wearing a U of S athletic shirt asked her.

Melissa froze. Didn't she know this person?

Wasn't she the tall girl on the basketball team who got benched last winter with a badly sprained ankle?

"Um," the girl repeated politely, "may I help you?"

Melissa leaned forward on her elbows. "Yes," she practically whispered, glancing behind her. "I, um, have an appointment."

"Okay." The girl nodded. "Who is your appointment with?"

"Dr. Penrose."

"Oh, yes. Dr. Penrose is over in mental health," the girl said loudly.

Melissa cringed.

"Take this hall down to the end and turn right. Check in there."

"Thanks," Melissa mumbled, moving away so that she was able to keep her face to the wall. In just a few seconds, she'd be away from the large reception area.

"Melissa!" she heard a familiar voice cry out behind her. Melissa stopped and turned around slowly. It was Winnie.

Melissa felt the blood rise up to her face. Nervous sweat broke out on her forehead. She was trapped. Trapped with Winnie, her kind but loudmouthed former roommate, in front of dozens of other students. "Hi," Melissa said hurriedly.

"Hi!" Winnie said, running her hand tiredly through her ragged, spiky hair.

Melissa paused. Winnie looked terrible. Her face was deathly pale, she had circles under her eyes, and her body looked thin and tired under her plain white tank top and jeans. Was she seeing things, or did Winnie look different because she wasn't dressed in one of her usual, weird fashion experiments?

"Uh," Winnie gasped, lowering her head down to her waist, as if she were trying to get her breath. Then she gave Melissa an embarrassed smile and fiddled nervously with the strap of her oversize neon-pink book bag. "I've been sick for a while."

Melissa nodded. "You don't look so good."

Winnie reached a hand up to her face. "I don't? I really don't? God. I'm here for blood tests. I hate needles. I hate the way they dab your arm with that little ball of cotton soaked in alcohol and poke around for your vein and . . . oh . . ."

"Are you okay?" Melissa asked as Winnie suddenly sat down on a nearby chair.

Winnie was fanning her face nervously with a notebook she'd pulled out of her bag. "Yeah.

Yeah. It's nothing." A smile stole over her face. Then Winnie pointed at her and started to give her a knowing smile. "I know why you're here."

Melissa stiffened.

"Josh told me you were going to come in for some counseling," Winnie said loudly, causing two girls from Melissa's chemistry class to look at them both as they walked past them in the hall.

Melissa wanted to crawl into a closet and die.

"I think it's *great*," Winnie continued, oblivious to Melissa's discomfort. Melissa watched as Winnie unfastened the top button on her jeans and let out a sigh of relief. "We've all been worried about you. We never see you. But this is a great first step. Which doctor is your appointment with?"

Melissa looked at her. She and Winnie had been roommates for many months before Winnie had married Josh. Winnie had put her through a lot. But she had never hated Winnie. She had never hated her the way she did that very moment.

"Counseling?" Melissa acted confused. "Doctor? I'm doing great. I don't know why everyone thinks I'm not."

Now Winnie looked confused.

"I'm here to cancel an appointment for a sprained tendon," Melissa lied.

"Oh."

"Yeah, I thought I sprained it during practice, but I guess I didn't, because it's fine now," Melissa went on boldly.

Winnie was staring at her with disbelief. "Oh, well—I'm glad to hear it."

"Thanks!" Melissa said airily, waving her hand and sailing down the hall and out the back exit. Once outside, she took a small sip of fresh air, then a larger one. She began walking rapidly, then faster, toward the gym. Clenching her jaw, she felt the strength in her legs beneath her warm-up pants.

The closer she got to the gym, the better she felt. It was almost like coming home. At least it was something familiar. Something she understood.

Out there on the track, she thought, *I don't have to explain anything. I don't have to expose my private feelings to strangers. And I don't have to rely on anyone but myself. It's just me and my body and a tiny part of my brain that tells me when to go and when to stop.*

Melissa broke into a light jog. All that mattered now was action. Running and winning. It had gotten her this far. It was the only thing she could count on now. Nothing was going to stop her from being the best now.

Nothing.

Sixteen

"**T**his meeting will come to order," said the Dean of Students, Harvey Scribner, as he thumped a wooden gavel and frowned at the packed hearing room.

Courtney sat tall and erect at a small table facing the dean. Next to her sat KC. Eric Sutter roamed the back of the room, looking confident and making a point of shaking hands with everyone he recognized.

"Will someone *please* shut the door?" Mr. Scribner said in a loud voice. His bald head was beginning to turn pink with impatience. Pushing his black-rimmed glasses up on his nose, he began shuffling anxiously through a pile of papers in front of him.

Courtney stirred in her seat and slipped her hand across the back of her neck. It was a hot spring afternoon, and the small, west-facing room was already stifling. Clumped together in the back of the room was a packed assortment of reporters, sorority sisters, feminists, and student leaders. She glanced quickly back, and for an instant saw Lauren give her a challenging glare.

"These personnel matters are normally closed to the public," Dean Scribner said irritably, running his finger under his tight shirt collar. "But both parties have asked for an open hearing, so we'll just have to do our best."

Courtney's eyes slid around the room. Eric was sitting down with a no-problem air, holding his hand up in greeting to a member of the board of regents who'd just entered the room.

Courtney's stomach felt sick with revulsion. His face wore the same fake smile it had worn the night before when she'd tried to talk to him— and ended up getting attacked instead. She knew he'd lie to the dean just like he'd lied to her. Just like he must have lied to a thousand people before this day.

"Uh, yes," Mr. Scribner mumbled. Then he

cleared his throat uncomfortably. "This is a fact-finding hearing. According to this university's policy, I will make a report to the affirmative action officer handling this case. The final decision will be rendered by the University of Springfield's sexual—uh—harassment panel."

Courtney watched as the dean nodded and smiled knowingly in Eric's direction.

"Miss Courtney Conner?" Dean Scribner looked down impatiently at Courtney over his glasses.

Courtney nodded. There was something about Dean Scribner's body language that made her feel like a schoolgirl who'd been dragged in on a fibbing charge. She was beginning to wonder if she should have insisted on a private investigation after all.

No, Courtney thought, holding her head up proudly. *I was the one who brought this out into the open. That's where it should stay. Even if nothing happens, at least it will make women more aware that they can be harassed—and by men they least expect it from.*

"Uh, yes," Scribner ran on. "Miss Courtney Conner has alleged that Mr. Eric Sutter has made unwelcome advances to her in the course of her internship with him. And that Mr. Sutter here has threatened to grade her poorly and file negative references if she uh . . . did not comply.'"

There was a loud murmur in the room, and the dean looked even more uncomfortable.

"He doesn't want to be here," KC hissed in Courtney's ear.

Courtney nodded. Scribner didn't look very sympathetic, but he had a job to do. According to KC, universities were worried about getting sued for this kind of thing, so most of them had new systems for dealing with sexual-harassment complaints.

"This hearing is a joke," KC continued to whisper angrily. "It's rigged for Eric."

"Ah-hem," Dean Scribner cleared his throat again and tugged at his rumpled vest. "Let me say that we here at the U of S are extremely disappointed to hear of these shocking charges. But we are pleased that Mr. Sutter has been willing to deal with it so openly." He nodded and smiled approvingly in Eric's direction. "So we'll go ahead now and try to get to the bottom of this."

"I don't like him," KC whispered. "I bet he'd love to squelch the whole thing."

"Miss Conner," Dean Scribner said sternly. "I'll give you a chance to make an opening statement. Then I may have questions for you."

Courtney took a deep breath and glanced over at

KC, who gave her an encouraging smile. "Thank you, Dean Scribner," she began steadily. "I'm glad to have the opportunity to air these charges. Over the course of my internship with Mr. Sutter, he has repeatedly approached me with suggestions that I become personally involved with him."

There was a loud snicker in the back of the room.

Courtney looked down and tried to concentrate. Then she looked up again. "I have refused Mr. Sutter's attentions each time. And I have told him that it's my work on the university's budget issues that I'm interested in . . . not romantic involvement."

A loud, muffled snort burst out behind her. Instinctively, Courtney turned around, only to have a camera-flash pop in her eyes.

Dean Scribner had an impatient look on his face. He removed his eyeglasses and tiredly rubbed his eyes. "Yes, yes, go on, Miss Conner."

"Since then, Mr. Sutter has threatened to give me a failing grade," Courtney continued. "And write a poor letter of recommendation for my transcript."

Courtney paused, unsure of what to say next. She'd filed written testimony, but she wanted to explain in detail the embarrassing way he had pinned her against the door of his office. The way he'd practically torn her shirt off the night before.

"Miss Conner?" Dean Scribner urged her on. "Anything else?"

She heard soft giggles in the back of the room. Then laughter and whispering. Instead of feeling indignant and courageous, Courtney was beginning to feel silly and ashamed.

Bravely, Courtney continued, trying to explain Eric's bizarre behavior, but feeling worse by the minute. Everything in her background told her that nice girls weren't supposed talk about these things.

The more details she revealed, the more the crowd snickered. And the worse she felt.

Finally, it was over. Courtney looked across and saw Eric shaking his head in disgust.

"Thank you, Miss Conner," Dean Scribner said distractedly, shuffling through a pile of papers. "Now—uh—we have a number of letters here written on your behalf. Mm hmm. I see that you are the president of the Tri Beta sorority. Letter from vice-president Diane Woo. Mm hmm, very nice."

Courtney spoke up. "I believe my advisor, Professor Adams, has submitted written testimony on my behalf."

Mr. Scribner shook his head and fingered the pile. "Noo. No Dr. Adams." Then, as Courtney's heart sunk further, he held up a letter and nodded his head. "Yes. Now I did have a question about this testimony. Mr. Dash Ramirez? Assistant editor for the U of S *Weekly Journal?*

Courtney felt something cave in inside.

"Now, Mr. Ramirez here testifies that you repeatedly harassed *him* over the course of several weeks. In fact, Mr. Ramirez is quite worried about you and feels that you are under some kind of emotional stress."

Courtney opened her mouth to say something, then closed it. There was silence, then a giggle in the back of the room.

"Miss Conner? You have a right to respond to these comments."

Slowly, Courtney turned her head around and scanned the small crowd. Dash wasn't even in the hearing room. Didn't he even have the guts to show his face?

All she could see were her grim-looking sorority sisters, a few news reporters with their pens eagerly poised, and rows of faces she didn't recognize, who were either shaking their heads in disgust, or trying to control their laughter.

KC was nudging her. "Don't pay any attention

to them. Just tell the truth and don't be afraid," she whispered.

Courtney shook her head. It was no use. This was just a freak show now. She knew no one believed her—and no one wanted to find out what really happened. Eric was too powerful. Even the women in the room didn't seem to believe what had happened to her.

Suddenly, Courtney heard the door to the hearing room open. She glanced up and felt the blood drain from her face. Dash and Cody walked in, breathing hard and looking around the room anxiously.

"Excuse me," she heard Dash say.

"I'm sorry," Mr. Scribner protested, trying to wave them away, "but we have important business in here today."

"We have some important evidence," Dash interrupted, striding up the aisle, followed by Cody, who slipped into a seat along the wall.

Courtney watched in horror as Dash pushed a white envelope onto the dean's front table. Dash had already incriminated her. What more could he possibly have to say? How much more was she expected to take?

"Please read this, Dean Scribner," Dash said urgently, his eyes darting in Courtney's direction.

"I think you'll find the contents of the envelope very interesting."

Josh burst into the health center's reception area and cast his eyes around frantically for Winnie. He'd barely slept the last two nights, and his eyes were like rocks in his head.

Since Winnie had agreed to see a doctor the night before last, his head had been buzzing with terrifying fantasies of Winnie in the hospital. Winnie on the operating table. Winnie having treatments.

He knew he'd go crazy if he didn't know soon what was wrong with her.

"Win!" he practically yelled when he saw her slumped in a corner couch, reading *Psychology Today* magazine and blowing her nose dejectedly. He unhooked his bike helmet, slipped his book bag off his shoulder, and sat down in the chair next to her. "What's going on?"

Winnie's eyes went up to the ceiling, exasperated. "First they made me wait half naked in a scary-looking room for an hour with no magazine . . ."

"Win. What . . ." Josh tried to interrupt.

"Then a strange nurse examined me, weighed me, felt my glands, and asked me boring questions about my diet and sleep habits," Winnie continued, slamming the magazine shut and slapping it on the table. "Then they sent me to an even scarier-looking place and proceeded to jab me with a large needle until they had extracted a very large quantity of my precious blood."

"But . . ."

"Then I fainted and fell, cutting the inside of my lip with my tooth." Winnie angrily pulled her lip down.

"Oh, Win. But . . ." Josh tried again.

"Then they sent me into a bathroom and made me pee into an extremely small paper cup. Then I had to walk down a hall and give another strange person my *urine*."

Josh's heart was beating. "Gee, Win. It sounds awful. But what did they . . ."

"It was humiliating."

"But what did they say?"

"They said nothing," Winnie declared, her spiky hair shaking with frustration. "Except, 'Please have a seat in the reception area. Dr. Johnson will call you'."

"Oh." Josh sighed. He looked at her thin body. "Did—did they look nervous or anything? I mean, did they say anything that would worry you?"

"No."

"Winifred Gottlieb. Please return to Waiting Area B. Winifred Gottlieb. Please return to Waiting Area B," a microphone blared.

"Okay. Okay," Winnie said irritably. "I heard you the first time."

Josh picked up his book bag and helmet and followed Winnie wearily down the hall. She looked so small in her tank top. Her hair was all bunched up and weird in the back, too. *She's so sick she probably isn't even aware of it,* Josh thought miserably.

"Winnie Gottlieb?" a woman with short, dark hair in a white coat asked pleasantly, extending her hand.

"Yes. Hello," Winnie mumbled.

"I'm Diane Johnson. I'll be seeing you today." She gave Josh a friendly look. "Are you a friend?"

"I'm Josh Gaffey, her husband," Josh said quietly, a catch in his throat.

"Oh, well then, I think you'd better come with me too."

Josh's heart froze. Something was stuck in his throat. Why did the doctor especially want him to come in too? Was it bad news? Was it one of those medical situations where it was necessary to have a family member present? What in the hell was happening?

"I hope that's all right," Dr. Johnson asked.

Josh coughed. "Oh. Sure," he spoke up, following Winnie and the doctor down the hall. His legs felt like lead. He needed to sit down.

"Please come in and have a seat," Dr. Johnson said, smiling and graciously motioning them into a small, paneled office covered with framed medical degrees, poster art, and family pictures.

"Are you going to examine me?" Winnie asked, taking a seat.

Dr. Johnson looked serious. "No. I don't think that will be necessary." She sat down comfortably in a large chair and looked thoughtfully at Josh and Winnie. "Have you been married long?"

Josh smiled shyly and took Winnie's hand. "Just a few weeks. But we've been together much longer than that, huh, Win?"

Winnie gave Josh a weak smile. "Love at first sight, orientation week. But then we had fights. You know. On and off and on and off and on and off and . . ."

Josh looked at Dr. Johnson, who was beginning to look as if she wanted to get down to business.

He turned and shook his head gently at Winnie, who immediately stopped talking.

"We've already run a battery of blood and urine tests," Dr. Johnson began. "Your symptoms are pretty classic, actually. Although that nasty bruise on your leg is unrelated, Winnie. That fall you took last week must have been a terrible one."

Winnie looked confused.

"Well," Josh began, his heart breaking. "Is—is it something you can take care of? I mean, is it curable?"

Winnie leaned forward urgently. "Just give it to us straight. We need to know what's going on. I mean, is there anything you can do for me?"

Dr. Johnson smiled and leaned back. "Winnie, you aren't ill at all."

"I certainly am," Winnie shot back. "I'm sicker than a dog. I've never been sick a day in my life and now I'm ready to check into the hospital and—"

"Winnie," the doctor interrupted. "You're not sick."

Josh held his breath.

"You're pregnant. About four weeks along."

Josh couldn't breathe. It was impossible to speak. He turned his head toward Winnie just as she turned to him. Together, their eyes widened in total and utter shock.

He was the same Josh and she was the same Winnie. But suddenly everything—*everything* in their lives had changed forever.

Seventeen

"**W**hat saddens me," Eric Sutter said, his voice rising with conviction, "is that women of real integrity and sincerity on this campus will be the ones who are harmed by Miss Conner's unfounded accusations."

Courtney bent her head down tiredly into her hands. Half an hour ago, Eric had launched into a dramatic and poetic self-defense that had silenced the entire hearing-room audience.

"The chilling effect this will have on professional working relations between men and women cannot be measured," Eric continued, his voice tinged with sorrow.

Courtney shook her head, then stared absently at the handsome shape of his head. The noncommittal gray of his suit. The shiny gleam of his shoes and his watch.

Eric Sutter was the sort of man she'd been trained all her life to trust. He could have been a young doctor. An aspiring lawyer. A friend of her father's.

And yet here was a man who had callously harassed and threatened her—without a thought to the way it could affect her professional reputation for the rest of her life.

"I bear this intelligent young woman no ill will," Eric said with a proud air of self-restraint. Courtney felt slightly ill as she watched Eric's blue eyes slide her way. She could feel a trickle of sweat threading its way down her back, beneath her blue suit and silk blouse. "I understand how difficult it can be to form an emotional attachment that's not returned."

Courtney cringed. KC was crossing and re-crossing her legs restlessly in the seat next to hers.

"I know, because it's happened to me," Eric added, nodding his head sadly.

She looked up. Dean Scribner's eyes were glued on Eric. Courtney thought the dean almost looked on the verge of tears.

"Give me a break," KC hissed furiously.

"But Miss Conner's emotional problems cannot take priority to the important work this university is endeavoring to accomplish—work that will affect the lives of thousands of students." Eric raised his voice slightly. "It would be easy for me to back off, pretend that I took advantage of this young woman, and let the issue fall by the wayside while I attend to other problems at other institutions. But I won't stand by and let it happen."

Courtney slumped slightly in her chair. She could hear the silence in the room. She glanced back and could see that even Diane Woo and her other sorority sisters were nodding quietly, as if they actually believed Eric.

"Thank you, Mr. Sutter," Dean Scribner said quietly. "Is that the conclusion of your testimony?"

Eric nodded solemnly. "Yes it is, sir."

Dean Scribner cleared his throat. "Oh yes, we have one more witness today before we adjourn." Flipping through his papers, he pulled out the white envelope Dash had placed on the table earlier. He opened it. "Mr. Dash Ramirez?"

Courtney stiffened in her hard wooden chair as Dash walked to the front of the room and sat facing the crowd. Her head was reeling. What had she done to make her life take this sharp turn for the worse? Why was Dash so intent on destroying her?

She watched as Dean Scribner read the contents of Dash's envelope. There was definitely something incriminating in it, Courtney thought miserably, watching the dean's eyebrows shoot up with shock and surprise.

What new crime have they invented for me now? Courtney wondered bitterly. *I should have just dropped the charges.*

Then the dean shook his head in disbelief. "Go ahead, Mr. Ramirez. I've read your written testimony."

Courtney watched with alarm as Dash's dark eyes fixed on her. "Last night, while visiting a neighbor of Mr. Sutter's," Dash began steadily, "I clearly overheard Mr. Sutter harass and physically attack Courtney Conner."

There was a collective gasp in the hearing room.

"Courtney apparently visited him last night in an attempt to reason with him." Dash turned and began glaring at Eric. "Eric Sutter plainly admitted his guilt and said that he would never admit it to anyone. When she tried to leave, he attacked her."

Courtney felt the blood rushing to her face. Tears of joy and relief were spilling down her face. Dash had overheard them last night!

The dean nodded approvingly at Dash. "Please go on, young man."

"Of course, Sutter's neighbor, Cody Wainwright, and I had no way of proving this actually happened last night," Dash continued, breathless. "But we did a little checking up on Mr. Sutter's record at other universities."

Courtney's mouth dropped open. One of the Tri Betas gasped. There was a loud stirring in the audience. She looked over at Eric, who had paled and was anxiously gripping the sides of his table. A tiny bead of sweat began rolling down his neck.

"Does the name Robin Trimble ring a bell?" Dash glared at Eric. "How about Nancy Cartwright? Katherine Norville?" Then he turned to the dean as Eric's jaw dropped in horror. "As I've outlined in my written testimony, all of these women have filed sexual harassment charges against Eric Sutter in the past year. And in all of these cases, the women were university students who had been chosen by him for internships while he worked as a university consultant."

Courtney clamped her hand to her mouth. She hadn't been the only one.

"Unfortunately," Dash continued, "in all three cases, the cases were either dismissed for lack of evidence—or the women dropped the charges."

"They were lying!" Eric cried out. "Those charges were completely unfounded!"

"Yes, yes, I see," Dean Scribner muttered, looking sternly at Eric, then back down at Dash's written testimony. "And I understand that Mr. Sutter waged a pretty tough fight in all of these cases."

Dash nodded. "It got pretty nasty, I guess."

The dean looked up at Dash with appreciation. "Thank you very much, Mr. Ramirez. I will follow up on this testimony."

After Dash finished speaking and stood up, Courtney could feel her face flush, but she kept her eyes on Dash. Their eyes locked briefly as he passed, and she could see that his face was tight with guilt.

"Thank you," Courtney whispered. And as he walked away, she could see that he was giving her a subtle 'okay' sign with his hand behind his back.

A few moments later, Dash was collapsing into a small chair in the back of the stuffy hearing room. The harassment hearing was over and Dean Scribner was stirring in his seat, waiting for the noise in the room to settle.

"That's all, then," Dean Scribner said gruffly, pounding his gavel for quiet. "I will submit my report to the university's affirmative action officer within ten days. After that, the U of S's sexual-harassment panel will make the final decision."

Dash sighed and closed his eyes with relief. It had been a hectic few hours. Early that morning, he and Cody had tracked down a member of the board of regents, who had dug up Eric Sutter's resumé of university consulting jobs. Within minutes, he and Cody were on the phone, calling university student-affairs officials all over the country.

It hadn't been really that hard to find the pattern. Eric Sutter always established student internships when he worked on college campuses. And all of the women who'd filed the harassment complaints had belonged to sororities. No doubt Eric figured that sorority girls were too nice and proper to stick with the nasty business of a sexual-harassment complaint. And he had been right. But that had been before he met Courtney Conner.

Once Dash and Cody had the information they needed, they had rushed back to the newsroom to write the testimony up.

They had arrived at the hearing just in time.

Dash shook his head and stared down at his worn jeans. Because of Courtney's courageous move—and the pattern of harassment he and Cody had uncovered—Eric Sutter would almost certainly face charges at the U of S.

Courtney might have acted like a crazy school-girl with him. But now he knew he'd always respect her for what she did today.

"Hey," Cody clapped his hand on Dash's shoulder as he left. "Good work."

Dash lifted his hand up for Cody to slap. "Thanks for the help. Couldn't have done it without you."

Cody smiled and shook his head as he moved down the aisle. "Yeah, you could have. You'd have done just fine."

Now that the hearing was adjourned, the noise level in the room was deafening. Everyone was talking at once. Chairs and tables were scraping and rumbling against the floor. Flashbulbs were popping. Eric Sutter had left quickly, but Courtney had been swarmed by a crowd of admirers.

Dash smiled. In a few minutes, he'd have to run back to the *Journal* newsroom and begin writing up the story.

Then he looked up.

Lauren was staring coldly down at him. Wearing a black T-shirt and a pair of camouflage pants, she looked like a guerrilla soldier who'd suddenly sneaked up on him in battle. One hand was planted on her hip, the other held a sharp pencil.

Dash started to get up. "Lauren."

"You always were good at digging up information—when your heart was in it," Lauren said, coolly chewing the eraser tip.

Dash felt his face go white. "When my heart . . . ?"

Lauren blew up. "You know what I'm talking about!"

Dash almost started to laugh. "Are you kidding?"

Lauren flung her pencil into the oversize bag that hung from her lean shoulder. "You're good. You're very good. You say that you don't care about Courtney anymore. Then you spend the entire morning calling people long-distance, desperately searching for someone who'll help her."

"She was unfairly accused," Dash shot back. "No way was I going to stand around and let a jerk like Eric Sutter get off."

"You sure went to a lot of trouble."

Dash couldn't believe his ears. People filing out of the room were staring at them.

"Don't you think creeps like Sutter should be exposed?" Dash asked her. "Can't you forget your personal feelings for a moment and recognize Courtney's courage? She stood up to him. Many women wouldn't have the guts."

"Plenty of the women I know would," Lauren replied quietly.

"Good." Dash rocked back and forth nervously on his heels. By this time, the room was empty.

"Look," Lauren said after a long silence. "This isn't working."

Desperate, Dash tried to contain the wild thumping inside of his chest. "What do you mean?"

"I mean it's not working between us," Lauren said simply. "I can't keep seeing you. I don't trust you."

"Lauren."

"I'm sorry. We can still work together." Lauren shrugged. "But the personal relationship is off. I can't handle it. I don't know if I'll ever be able to."

Eighteen

"**A**re you going to be all right?" KC asked Courtney, who was sprawled happily on her pink bed in the Tri Beta house, taking another congratulatory call on the telephone. Surrounding her were a half dozen of her closest Tri Beta sisters.

Courtney pressed a hand to the receiver and looked up. A shiny sweep of her blond hair fell back. Her cheeks were rosy with happiness and her eyes were shining. "Thanks, KC. Thanks for sticking by me. I'll never forget it."

KC gave her a corny smile and bowed. "What are friends for?"

Courtney grabbed a pillow and threw it at her, laughing. "Right. Now get out of here and finish that western civ paper."

"Whatever you say," KC mocked, shutting the door just in time to avoid a flying teddy bear.

Since Courtney's surprise victory at the hearing that afternoon, the Tri Beta house had been in one long giddy celebration. But as KC walked out into the dark spring night, she grew thoughtful. Her long hair rustled in the warm breeze. She could feel her skirt swirl around her legs and hear the distant laughter of boaters down at Mill Pond.

What Courtney had done was truly amazing. In the face of terrible obstacles, she had stood up for herself. She had stuck to the truth about Eric Sutter and never backed down.

There was a clicking sound behind her on the path and KC instinctively moved over to make room for the coasting bicyclist.

"Hey," a deep voice murmured in the dark. KC turned and felt a pang. It was Cody, slowing his bike down and gracefully slinging his long leg over the crossbar. Still hanging on to the handlebars, he began walking next to her.

"Hi," KC said shyly. After her last confrontation with Cody in her dorm room, she didn't know if he'd ever speak to her again.

For a while, the only sound between them was the steady clicking of his bike chain as they moved down the path together. It felt good to have Cody there next to her, but she really didn't know what to say.

"Some hearing," he finally said. KC looked over. His long hair was pulled back into a ponytail that shone even in the darkness. It fell back over his brown leather vest. His white shirt matched the whiteness of his teeth. Just looking at him made her heart go weak.

"Yes."

"Courtney's something," Cody said softly. "I misjudged her."

"Thanks for standing up for her," KC said slowly, twisting a strand of her hair. "The research you and Dash did this morning saved her."

"Sure."

KC gave Cody a guilty look. "Look, I'm sorry about the other day."

"Oh, that."

"I mean," KC said slowly, "about telling you I was interested in you just to get back at Peter. I guess I just said it out of spite. I was angry when you didn't support Courtney like I wanted you to."

KC watched Cody absently push his bike forward, catch it, and push it out again with his hand. "One thing you have to understand about me, KC," Cody began softly, "is that I act on the truth when I see it. I know that sounds a little preachy. But it's just something that my dad and I talked about a lot. I guess it's been passed down to me."

"My dad, too," KC whispered. "It was everything to him."

Cody pointed to the carved silver bracelet on his forearm. "Cherokee."

"Oh," KC murmured.

"My dad—he's Cherokee," Cody continued. "He always gave it to everyone straight. It was important to him."

KC looked over and saw that he was looking at her intently. "What is it?"

"I guess I'm expecting a little truthfulness from you," Cody said, shrugging impatiently.

"You don't think I'm being . . . ?"

"No."

"You mean about Peter?"

"That's right."

KC listened to the sound of her shoes against the path. The clicking of the bike. The crickets in the bushes beside them. She heard distant laughter and splashing in the distant pond. Everything seemed so peaceful and right at that moment, walking there with Cody. It was as if he'd melted her down to the point where she wasn't afraid anymore. Not of the truth about Peter, or of the truth about her own feelings.

"Well," KC began carefully, "I did call Peter in Italy the other night and found out through a housemate that he's seeing another girl."

"Uh-huh."

KC drew her breath in, then let it out. It felt good. "I was angry," she admitted. "I was furious. I don't know. I guess I was hurt, but I was also sad. He meant a lot to me, and now he's gone."

"He is?"

"Yeah, I think he is."

"And you weren't the one calling the shots on that, were you, KC?" Cody said softly. KC shivered when she felt his arm slip around her shoulders. "That made you angry too, didn't it."

"Yes, it did," KC answered, her eyes filling with tears. "I guess you could say I'd rather be the betrayer than the betrayed. It's one of my faults."

"I forgive you."

"Anyway," KC said, gently touching the tips of Cody's fingers on the top of her arm. "I guess in one way, I threw myself at you to get back at Peter. But there was more to it than that."

"Glad to hear it."

KC stopped in the middle of the path, listening to a pair of Canada geese honking overhead. Then she looked up at the inky blue sky. "I really do like you, Cody. I want to be closer to you."

KC felt Cody's fingertips slip down over her hand as he gently lowered his bike onto the grass. He pulled her around toward him. Then she felt his chest against hers and his hand stroking her back. His face was dipping down to kiss her.

"You got it, KC."

Glasses clinked. Laughter rang out. The Tri Betas' elegant living room was decorated with floral arrangements, ribbons, and tiny celebratory balloons.

"May I have your attention, everyone?" Diane Woo called out over the happy gathering. She clinked a spoon against her crystal glass for quiet.

Courtney stood proudly in front of the elegant Tri Beta fireplace as her sorority sisters gathered around. As she scanned their faces, she saw that they no longer held expressions of embarrassment and suspicion. She saw respect, even admiration.

"Come on, everyone," Diane called out cheerfully. "I'd like to make a toast."

"Hear, hear," Stephanie Mills called out.

There was a rustling of skirts and napkins as the crowd quieted under a sparkling chandelier.

"What Courtney's been through over the last few weeks," Diane began, glancing at Courtney with a mixture of disbelief and pride, "well, I just hope none of us will ever have to go through ourselves."

Courtney beamed. It didn't even seem to matter that half of the girls there hadn't believed her harassment charges at first. Or that they'd been upset with her behavior over Dash. At least now they seemed to support her.

"But this is what I want to say to Courtney. Thanks for your courage. Thanks for having the guts it takes to fight for your self-respect. You didn't run. You didn't hide, even though it meant risking everything. You are a shining example to all of us."

Courtney smiled and nodded her thanks as the group broke out into applause. Then her expression turned serious. "Thanks, Diane. Thanks for helping me celebrate the end of the worst few weeks in my life."

There was a ripple of polite laughter.

"I hope none of you has to go through what I did with Eric Sutter," Courtney began. "But chances are that some of you will." Courtney gripped her glass tightly and took a breath.

"In a few years, many of you will be in professions where you will work closely with men—most of them good, some of them unscrupulous . . ."

There was a murmur of understanding.

"And some of them will be completely ignorant of how offensive their comments and attitudes can be to the women they work with."

Courtney stared hard into the faces of her sorority sisters. "What I want to say is this: If you run into unwelcome romantic passes—or even out-and-out threats on the job, as I did—try not to feel ashamed. And for god's sake, don't keep quiet about it. Speak out. Tell the guy it offends you, and if he doesn't stop, report it."

"Right!" someone called out from the back.

"It may be embarrassing," Courtney continued, her voice quavering slightly. "But men like Eric Sutter have no right to use their power in exchange for sex. No matter what."

Courtney felt Diane's arm slip around her waist, and suddenly, she was surrounded with hugs of congratulation. Then, out of the corner of her eye, she saw KC motioning to her and pointing toward the hall. Gently pulling herself away, she ducked away.

"What is it?" Courtney whispered.

KC shrugged. "It's Dash. He's in the front entry."

Courtney straightened herself and walked proudly down the carpeted hall until she saw him standing in front of an oil painting, nervously stroking his stubbly chin.

"Hi," Dash said, a little uncomfortably.

"I should be coming to thank you," Courtney said quietly. "What you did for me . . . well, I'll never be able to thank you enough."

Dash extended his hand. "Glad things worked out."

Courtney shook it. "You did some fast work."

He shrugged and looked down at the ragged toe of his hightop sneaker. "I've come to apologize, actually. Listen, Courtney. I'm sorry about that testimony against you. It's just that I thought you were going through some kind of an emotional crisis. And when I saw you that day in Sutter's office, it just looked like you two were—well, together. I should have listened to what you said. You've got guts. I don't think Sutter planned on that."

Courtney shrugged. "He should have picked on someone working in a corporation or a business without a strong harassment policy. The U of S is being really supportive."

"Good."

Courtney shook her head again. "If I'd known more about this problem, I would have recognized it earlier, instead of blaming myself. And I would have realized that I didn't necessarily have to go public. The U of S would have investigated it for me privately."

"Are you trying to give me a story idea for the *Journal*?" Dash teased.

"You bet I am," Courtney said seriously. "I'm planning to take this issue out into the open. Workshops. Forums. Newspaper articles. Anything. I want women to know that creeps like Sutter exist. And they don't have to put up with it."

"Let me know if I can help."

"Thanks, Dash." Courtney looked at him. "I'm sorry I put you through all that craziness. You know, when I wouldn't let go? I'm not sure what happened to me. But I went nuts, and I'm sorry."

"It's okay." Dash reached out and touched her chin gently, almost sadly.

Courtney stared at his dark eyes. They didn't seem so mysterious anymore. They didn't make her body go limp. And they didn't make her forget everything else. He was just Dash. Dash Ramirez the nice guy and the great reporter who saved her life.

She watched, her heart light, as he left slowly through the front door. Something had loosened in her heart, as if she'd tugged on a hard knot, finally untangling it. The tension, the self-doubt, the fear—it was all spilling out.

Then she realized that she was finally free. Free of Dash. Free of Eric Sutter. And free of her own self-doubt.

Here's a sneak preview of
Freshman Christmas, *the second*
book in the FRESHMAN DORM
super series.

"e have to find KC!" Winnie said, seeming close to tears. "She's with Jeremy Tower. One of the Tower twins!"

"You mean that super hunk she was dancing with is a Tower?" Faith gasped. "I wonder if she knows it."

"She couldn't possibly," Winnie said. "Not from the big love looks she was giving him. Jake Tower's fiancée told me the old man will bust a gut if he sees them together."

"Well, where did she go?" Kimberly asked.

"I don't know. One minute she was right in

front of me and then I looked away for a second—
to check if any bouncers had stopped you guys—
and when I looked back, she was gone. I don't see
her anywhere! Now the Towers are on to us. We
have to find KC and leave."

"You're right, it's better out here," KC said as
she and the cowboy she'd just met walked away
from the barn.

"I'm not a lover of crowds," he said. "I can only
stay a little while at a party, and then I need to
breathe."

KC gazed up at his dark eyes. She saw in them a
passionate intensity tinged with a rebellious spirit.
In all her life she'd never felt such an instant connection to anyone.

"I've seen you before, you know," she told him.

He pushed up his scruffy cowboy hat. "Is that
so? Where?"

"On that rodeo poster in The Hungry Horse."

She melted as he smiled softly. "It's a fool thing
to do, but I love it," he said. "There's so little
you can control in this world. And a bucking
bronco is one thing I can. I get a real rush every-
time I stay on."

"Isn't it terribly dangerous?" KC asked, suddenly

feeling a deep pang at the thought of anything happening to him.

"The danger is part of the appeal," he admitted, taking a seat on a wooden fence railing. "There would be no excitement to the thing if it was safe. The next step is bull riding. Now there's a creature that is dead set against having anything on its back. It's the nature of the beast. I've signed up for the first bull-riding event at the Christmas rodeo."

KC felt a powerful urge to touch him and she put her hand on his arm. "I'd hate to see you get hurt."

"I won't get hurt. I'm indestructible," he said, laughing with a note of sad irony. "What I'd really like to do is run a ranch. I'd be damn good at it, too. I almost had a shot at it once, but things got screwed up."

"Things have a way of doing that," KC said sympathetically. Their eyes locked. KC was aware of her heart pounding triple fast and wondered if he could hear it.

"You are so beautiful," he murmured. "I noticed you right away."

She leaned into him, feeling like a flower moving toward the sun. And then his arms were around her and his lips were on hers. She slid her hands along the back of his neck and kissed him with as much deep longing and urgency as she sensed coming from his whole body.

Then somehow they turned, and KC was now backed up against the fence. He leaned against her, he ran his fingers through her long hair, all the while kissing her hungrily.

KC didn't want him to stop. She didn't want the moment to end. But faraway voices floated into her consciousness. Then the voices got closer. Were there people nearby? It didn't matter. Nothing mattered but him.

"I said let that little tramp go!" a male voice boomed.

This time there was no ignoring it. Still holding her, the cowboy turned. Over his shoulder, KC saw Lewiston Tower, Jake Tower, and a blond woman.

"Is there a problem, grandfather?" the cowboy asked.

"Grandfather!" KC gasped. She looked at him in disbelief. "Lewiston Tower is your relative?"

"One hundred percent right, young lady," Lewiston Tower answered, his eyes boring into KC. "And let me tell you that gate-crashers are not welcome at my party. Your behavior is not only disrespectful and brazen—but shameful.

Then again, I guess one can't expect much more from someone with your family name."

KC's jaw dropped, but no words came out. She was too stunned and confused. She looked from grandfather to grandson. "Who are you?" she managed to ask.

"Jeremy Tower," the cowboy replied, his eyes searching her face. "Who are *you*?"

"Oh, this is rich!" Jake Tower sneered before KC could respond.

"Shut up, Jake," Jeremy snapped, stepping forward.

Jake laughed. "You fool! You've been here making out with one of the bitches from the Angel Ranch. She's an Angelleti."

KC watched Jeremy's strong hand curl into a fist as he lunged at his brother.

"Stop!" shrieked the blonde, jumping between them with her arms waving. "Stop it!"

"Get out of the way, Suzanna!" Jeremy shouted. But the woman stood her ground.

KC's head swam and she felt as if it was *her* Jeremy had punched. How could he be a Tower —part of the family that was trying to bring financial ruin on her mother? It was impossible. It couldn't be.

But it was true.

"There she is!" she heard Winnie shout. KC looked toward the barn and saw her friends coming out. As soon as they spotted her, they broke into a run.

"Excuse me," KC said with all the dignity she could muster. The warmth of Jeremy's kisses was still on her lips, but KC couldn't bring herself to look at him, even as she stepped past him and his brother.

"I won't forget this intrusion," Lewiston Tower shouted after her. "Next time, know that you don't belong."

And I won't forget your rudeness, KC thought bitterly, but she said nothing in return. Instead, she walked with her head held high until she met up with her friends by Kimberly's van.

"What happened?" Faith asked urgently.

"I'll tell you later," KC said, terrified that the tingling in her eyes would turn into tears at any moment. Right now, that would be the worst possible thing to happen. "Let's just get out of here, fast."